Terminated -
The Making of
a Serial Killer

TERMINATED - THE MAKING OF A SERIAL KILLER

VOLUME 2 - FROM HERO TO SERIAL KILLER

AARON AALBORG

Penman House Publishing

Published by Penman House Publishing

ISBN: 978-0-9908764-8-9

Typesetting services by BOOKOW.COM

To all those who have suffered from the greed and arrogance of bosses, politicians and others with no empathy. To all those in business, care-giving, administration and others who work for the benefit of all beings and the people they work with.

Acknowledgments

My thanks are due to the following:

For helpful comments on parts of the story: James Fraser, Professor Leo Murray, Dr. Lenny Karpman, David Truslow, Lucinda Gray, Carol Marujo, Kate Stanger, Richard Baksa and Paul "Fuzzlong" Furlong.

For support and much helpful advice, fellow novelists from Penman House Publishing: Mike Crump and K. Francis Ryan.

For editing: Bob Brashears.

For inspiration: The people I have worked and had fun with all over the world in the Royal Marines, marketing, accounting, consulting, academia, investment banking, executive search, various Buddhist groups and lots of sociopaths.

PROLOGUE

Terminated Volume 2 continues Alex McDonald's roller coaster ride through life. In Volume 1 we saw him rise from a dirt poor beginning, through the dangers and horrors of the Falklands War to great excitement and success, but with devastating personal consequences.

Volume 2 takes him onwards and upwards. Alex is plagued by sociopaths and corruption in all the businesses he works in. His moral code is challenged at every turn. Assignations and murders dog his steps. The CIA and British intelligence services plague his every move. He enjoys the heights of love and success and sees the depths of despair and failure.

The action takes place around the world, with many twists and turns. This all leads to an amazing and unexpected crescendo.

TERMINATE

"*All tremble at violence. All fear death. Putting oneself in the place of another, one should not kill or cause another to kill.*"

The Buddha

"*By three methods we may learn wisdom: first by reflection, which is noblest, second by imitation, which is easiest and third by experience which is bitterest.*"

Confucius

CHAPTER ONE

PTSD

"PTSD, (Post Traumatic Stress Disorder), results from unsuccessful attempts by the human psyche to bury horrific memories."

A Psychologist working with military veterans in New York

The weight of Alex's suspended body caused the chains to tear into his wrists. Helplessly, he dangled from a hook in the concrete ceiling. The hood was off. He glowered at his tormentors through the slits of his bloodied, swollen eyelids. He tried to banish the pain from his dislocated shoulders.

He spat blood towards the Argentinean officer. The man nodded at the corporal. Thwack! The rubber truncheon cracked a rib.

"You are not a Gringo. Where you from Mister?"

Thwack!

"You will talk."

Thwack!

"Everybody does."

Thwack!

"Tell me, then. And then this can end."

Alex heard an older voice from deep within his head. It was his father's rough Glaswegian accent.

"Remember this son. Never give up!"

Thwack!

Alex passed out.

He awoke on the hard floor of a chilly, pitch-black cell. He shivered in a cold fever. The Hessian sack was back over his head. The dust from the beans it once held smelled musty. He could feel the tight ropes binding his hands and feet. Cramps and pain wracked his body.

Random thoughts came and went. He remembered the sickening crack, as he wrenched a bodyguard's head around in the hotel in Buenos Aires. His strong hands twisted till the man's neck broke. He groaned. He had broken his martial arts code. He no longer used his skills only for self-defense. He was a killer.

Next, he became wracked with guilt over the death of his French ex-lover. They had a fling at the INSEAD business school. The scene of her death arose vividly. *Oh no! I pushed her.* The bus hit her with a sickening thud.

In his delirium, he saw his former wife, Morag's hospital bed in Liverpool. He seemed to be floating above it near the ceiling. She was dying, silently calling his name. He could not make her see him. His estranged daughters did not look up to him. Each held one of his wife's hands.

He had betrayed them all. His sexual dalliances and obsession with success had led to Morag's death. He clamped his eyes tight. Tears welled up.

He slipped into unconsciousness. Thud! An Argentinean soldier kicked him awake. His broken rib stabbed into him. He was raving. His heart pumped faster as the memories rushed in. He was running, skiing, hiding, shooting at an Argentinean plane. It was machine-gunning him. It crashed in a fireball.

Thud!

"You no sleep, señor."

The last word was a sneer.

Thud! Another kick, to his hip. He tried to use his Buddhist meditation to avoid the pain. He conjured his karate Sensei's voice.

"Pain is an illusion. It is only felt in the mind. We only think it comes from other parts of our body. Focus on the breath. It will pass."

Thud! It did not work. He remembered the water-boarding test in his Royal Marine training. Breathing was impossible. Racked with agony, he was drowning. He had to give them what they wanted—anything to make this stop.

The hood was on. He felt some things crawling about under the Hessian. They tickled his face. One walked across his eye. He blinked it shut. *Spiders? Ants? Centipedes? There must be hundreds of them.*

"Aaaieee!"

Thud, another kick. He felt hands shaking the hood. The crawling things started to sting and bite. They began to eat him alive. He felt one crawling inside his ear.

Desperately, he twisted and turned. He was drenched in sweat. He screamed and screamed.

* * *

Tenderly, she soothed his brow with a cool, damp cloth.

"Oh my love, you're having those nightmares again."

He struggled to sit up. His eyes flew wide open. He was safe in his bed in London. She was beautiful. His muscles relaxed. He sank back into the soft mattress with a groan. She gently took his hand and tenderly kissed his forehead.

She wondered again about his heavily scarred body and two missing toes. He clammed up whenever she asked. He obviously did not want to talk about it. He raised such conflicting emotions. *Who are you really Mister Alex McDonald?*

CHAPTER TWO

Girl on a Motorcycle

"Thundering down a shady tree-lined road, I flick to the outside and set up for a fast left-hander... maybe a bit too hot. Brake till I'm blue...feel the back lift.

"Now! I pitch it in—bike under immaculate tension at full lean and I'm just dragging the rear brake—don't dare more—front too, just keeping pressure as I use my thumb to roll the gas on. Easy for stability at first...adding more as the rear slips and catches—I know I have it now. I release the brakes altogether. I feel the front lift for the wheelie. Funny how thoughts pass... A tiny patch of rubber between me and the road. Damn I love my motorcycle!"

P. "Fuzzalong" Furlong lifelong motorcyclist and writer

Alex McDonald, former Major in Royal Marines, was hurtling north from London on the M1 motorway. The throaty growl from the huge engine penetrated his crash helmet. The wind howled around his face. The apparently antique motorbike he straddled was a 1955 Ariel Square Four. It raced along like a shiny black scorpion, dangerous and mean. Its rider stretched low over the tank, one with the machine. Slipstream tugged at his coal-dark leathers.

He mused on events since his return to London. Margaret Thatcher, the Prime Minister, stood for everything he despised: privilege, English domination and arrogance. Yet, she had personally thanked him, a Scot, for his contribution to the recent Falklands War.

In the year since then, he and his firm had been handsomely rewarded. Kendrick and Company, a top consulting partnership, was awash with important and hugely lucrative government assignments. His resentful rivals in the firm had tried to prevent his return. His critics were silenced, for now.

Currently, he was on top-secret activities for Ian Macgregor, the Scottish American who was brought in by Thatcher to fix the state owned British coal industry. It was fascinating work. Aspects of it caused him sleepless nights.

Bugger! He glanced over his shoulder, through his WORLD WARII pilot's goggles. He preferred them to modern Perspex visors. A police motorcycle with a white, fiberglass fairing was closing on him fast. He saw its flashing blue light in the outside lane. Now he could hear the siren.

Damn! He cut his engine on the hard shoulder. Sitting back, he pulled up his goggles, a picture of innocence.

The cop pulled over in front of him. He kicked down his stand with a long, black, leather riding boot. He strode over purposefully. He was tugging out a black notebook. He fixed Alex with a flinty stare. His voice was laced with that sarcasm and that false deference that all British cops learn.

"Do you know how fast you were going, *sir?*"

Alex smiled inside, keeping a straight face. It was a trick question. If he said "No," he could be charged with "driving without due care and attention." That was more serious than just speeding.

"About 80 officer. Look, I'm sorry, there was nobody around and I just wanted to try out my new bike."

"Actually, I could hardly catch you. It was 95 miles per hour!"

The cop now glanced admiringly at the gleaming Arial.

"Wow a Squarial! We don't see many of these around. How fast will it go?"

"Well I got a 105 out of her on the race track at Thruxton. With the mods, I think she can go faster."

Eyes gleaming, the cop bent to scrutinize the engine. "What have you done to it?"

"I had the cylinder head changed and special valves fitted."

Alex did not tell him about the other modifications. The serious money he was now earning had to go somewhere. This bike and his discretely grey, AC Ace sports car back in London; these were his pride and joy. His London bachelor pad was rather modest. His estranged daughters had returned the checks he sent them. What use was money to him?

"Listen, I promise to slow down officer. Can't you let me off this time?"

The policeman tucked his book back in his top pocket and put back on his stern face.

"All right, but we'll be watching out for you. Stick to the speed limit in the future!"

Alex breathed a sigh of relief. He remounted, kick-starting his bike. For a mile or two the cop trailed him. Then he peeled off at an exit ramp.

As the M1 became the A1, Alex accelerated to a steady 100 mph, relishing the wind in his face. He burned past other traffic. A couple of dozy drivers swerved unnecessarily in alarm, as he rocketed past.

* * *

Later that day, Alex was enjoying a pint of Theakston's Old Peculier at a roadside table. The pub, the Whitestonecliffe Inn, was an annual pit stop for bikers on the way to the big rally at nearby Duncombe Park in Yorkshire. The food here was always excellent and there was plenty of it. The landlord and his staff were friendly and welcoming. The bar maids were pretty. He would return.

The village had a 30 mph speed limit and some serious bends. Half a mile further on, there was an exciting one-in-four climb up the 500 foot limestone escarpment. It featured a snaking, narrow road with a couple of devil's elbows. Even the most powerful engines strained in low gears.

Alex tucked into his roast beef and Yorkshire pudding, enjoying the mellow English ale. He listened to his fellow bikers talking. A bumble-bee buzzed languidly around a geranium tub in the warm sunlight.

"These Jap machines are all very well, but our British motorcycle industry is really suffering. I'll stick with my Norton."

The speaker nodded lovingly towards his highly polished, silver-tanked machine in the row of parked bikes.

A man in worn black leathers, with a thick Liverpool accent, responded.

"I'm all for the British workers, but my Honda Gold Wing has disc brakes, an electric starter, indicator lights and goes like hell."

Another chimed in.

"BSA was the biggest manufacturer in the world. Triumph, Norton, Royal Enfield, Matchless, Velocette and others were all best sellers. Where are they now? We win the War and the bloody Japs take over the market."

Alex held his peace. Two sides to his character were always in conflict in such discussions. His family's working class background, made him sympathetic to people losing their jobs to foreign competitors. His brain and economics training was all for modernization, world trade and efficiency.

His father had witnessed Japanese atrocities in Burma. Unsurprisingly, he moaned a lot about how Japanese competition was closing down the Glasgow shipyards. Alex studied Karate under a Japanese sensei. He had learned restraint and built an indomitable inner strength. He was torn.

He thought, *Ha! The bloody English always talk about British when it suits them. They don't care about the decline in Scottish steel and shipbuilding. Well the Japanese need work too. Trying to stick with the old ways is like holding back the tide. It's compete or die.* This discussion about the motorcycle industry was all so very like his current dilemma over the UK coal industry.

As his silent reflections continued, he picked up a wonderful sound. Tiny at first, it grew louder. Suddenly, the rising roar of a speeding bike drowned out the bikers' chatter. They all looked up.

It burst into view, small in the distance but growing rapidly. Bright red, its rider was clad in all white leathers and helmet. It was doing least double the speed limit. They received an easy, gauntleted wave. A jab on the brakes made the front dive. A twist of the throttle created a perfect wheelie, right in front of them. Then, with a tremendous roar the bike heeled over.

It vanished round the next bend in a crescendo of sound. This faded, leaving a second's silence. A lamb bleated in a nearby field.

"Silly long haired sod!" grumbled one of the drinkers.

"Another flash foreign machine. The Wops lost the War too." Added another.

Alex was not listening. He admired the panache of the performance. He had considered buying a new 900 V-twin Ducati Darmah like this one. Maybe he should have? Still, discretion was more his style.

* * *

Later that afternoon, Alex slowly weaved his throatily burbling machine between the tents. Each had an adjacent motorbike. He found a quiet spot at the edge of the campsite. It was conveniently close to the showers and the bar tent. He pitched his one-man bivouac next to the Squarial. A few gawkers ambled over to admire it.

As the summer sunset lingered low over the knurled limbs of silhouetted oaks, he prepared to turn in. Then, a familiar red Ducati with its white leathered rider slowly laced its way through the throng towards him. The spot next to his tent was probably the last on the field.

The pale ghostlike figure sat up on the saddle. It lifted the dark visor and asked.

"Is it OK to squeeze in here?"

He was amazed. It was a girl. And an attractive one at that. She had a freckled face, with astonishing emerald eyes. Removing her helmet, she shook out her auburn hair. His heart beat faster.

"Of course, nice bike. You passed our pub around lunchtime."

Her eyes twinkled at him. "I saw you with all the fat old men."

"Can I help you pitch your tent?"

She bridled a little.

"No thanks. I'm a big girl now."

Mmm a feisty one. He watched as she expertly erected her tent. Unaware of her effect on Alex, she peeled of her leathers to reveal a tight T-shirt and shorts. She had a scorpion tattooed on a well toned shoulder. Her T-shirt read: "Handle With Care"

Right then, he thought.

"Now you've got that done, can I buy you a beer?"

She looked skeptically at him. Then she ran an appraising eye over his bike. He was good looking, in a tough sort of way. That was a hell of an interesting machine. There was something not quite right about it.

"OK for a beer, but I buy my own."

They sat in a couple of plastic chairs drinking from their bottles. They talked bikes.

"What have you done to that Squarial? It looks a little strange."

He smiled.

"I had an exact replica of the original frame made in titanium. The springs are flattened. The engine is an upgraded reproduction, cast in aluminum with steel cylinder sleeves. It's supercharged."

She was impressed. It must have cost a fortune though.

"How would you like to match me for a ride before breakfast?"

Surprised, he agreed.

* * *

In her lonely basement flat in London's Kensington, Dr. Maria Ramirez tossed and turned in her bed. She had thrown back the covers. Nonetheless, her gym-muscled body was bathed in sweat. The sheets were soaked.

Each day she coldly conducted her duties as a valued agent in Britain's, secret overseas intelligence service, MI6. She traveled extensively, especially to her native Gibraltar and to Latin America.

Maria relished the rare occasions when she could kill. Then, she had absolute power. They picked her for the toughest assignments, when her ruthless efficiency was required.

Nightly, she entered her other world of anger and frustration. It was always the same. She dreamt only of Alex. He had loved her, then defied her. He left her unconscious in a Buenos Aires hotel. *The bastard stole my mission, breaking all the rules. He disobeyed orders. He wriggled out of the consequences. He received the plaudits.*

She was blamed for letting him get out of control. He was an impulsive, insubordinate, handsome devil. He was a great lover. She loved him. She hated him. *One day, I'll screw him again. He'll fall in love with me. Then I'll kill him.*

* * *

At 5:00 am Becky Halstead, rider of the red Ducati, reached in through Alex's unlaced canvas tent flap. She tugged on a bare toe. She felt missing toes. It took her aback. *Maybe he came off his bike. That'd fit with the scar on his face.* She made a mental note to find out. He looked rough, but his eyes shone with friendly intelligence. *He speaks with an educated Scottish accent. He's interesting and funny. He doesn't wear a wedding ring.*

"Come on lazy bones. Are we up for that ride or what?"

He had spent an untroubled night for the first time in ages. No nightmares. He shook himself awake.

Fifteen minutes later, after a desultory wash in icy water, they rumbled over towards the entrance. At the gate to the camp, she laughed at the dawn. Slamming her visor down as she shouted,

"Come on I'll race you to the White Horse."

Rear wheel kicking up gravel, she disappeared with a thundering exhaust.

He hugged his gas tank for speed as he streaked after her. She weaved and leaned into the first corner. Her knee skimmed an inch above the unforgiving asphalt.

There was a long straight stretch of road. Consumed by the thrill of the chase, he turned full throttle. Gradually, he overhauled her. Her head turned toward him as he passed.

At the left turn from the main road, she made at crazy speed into the corner. She wobbled a couple of times and tweaked her throttle. She passed on his inside, almost forcing him off the road. He felt the bike slipping away beneath him. He tweaked more power. Adjusting the steering, he barely recovered. Furious, he roared after her.

She ignored the "No Motor Vehicles" sign at the cliff top path. An early morning dog walker leapt aside in fright. His dog yelped behind them. Their motors bellowed.

There's no room to pass her. He beat a balled fist on the handlebars in frustration. *Bluidy besom!*

Elated, she made it to the top of the White Horse ahead of him. This monolith was cut into the greensward of the escarpment. Pale limestone shaped the animal. From the flat plane below, it could be seen for miles.

He was still rather cross with her as he pulled up alongside.

"Hey you nearly killed me and yourself."

"Oh don't be silly. Come and get me."

She dropped her helmet and gloves by her bike and ran off. After a chase through the trees, he caught her. The sweat, the smell of warm leather as the studs and zips were torn open was electrifying. Frenziedly tossing aside their gear, they made sticky love in the grass. Ignoring the insect bites, they rolled over and over. They climaxed together. He collapsed, still clinging.

Utterly sated, she lit up a joint. She took a long languid drag between engorged lips. Then rolling her head back, she blew a perfect smoke ring. They watched it drift away. She held her spliff towards him.

"No thanks, I don't smoke."

She cast him a quizzical glance.

"Come on stuffy! There's more fun to be had."

Reluctantly, he took a long toke. He sat up coughing.

She laughed and laughed. They made love again, more slowly.

He felt a couple of swollen insect bites on his buttocks. Perhaps there were a few nettle stings as well.

"OK big boy, what's your name and where do you live?"

Her accent was educated. Maybe London. There was a smoker's, sexy tone.

"I'm Alex McDonald."

He held out an ironic hand for a shake as they sat side by side.

She took the hand with a broad grin as he continued,

"I live in Maida Vale, North London. How about you?"

"Rebecca Halstead, not at your service. You can call me Becky. I have a place in the East End."

"Will I see you again Becky Halstead?"

"You bet, but you'd best leave the flash machine elsewhere. The neighbors'll strip it for parts."

She pretty well ignored him for the rest of the rally, though she proffered her phone number. He wondered whether he would see her again. He was keen to try.

CHAPTER THREE

Class Warfare

"We need action not words. For the first time, we're facing the prospect of seeing legislation introduced. It will deny the right of trade unionists to come to the assistance of other unionists. It denies the right of trade unionists to seek the support of others in their disputes. There is only one response. Faced with this legislation, we say we will defy the law. It is the only action we can take. It is the only response this movement can give."

Arthur Scargill, union leader of UK miners

"The problem with socialism is that you eventually run out of other people's money."

Prime Minister Margaret Thatcher

Harris of MI6 and Roberts, his counterpart from MI5, were taking their weekly lunch in the Special Forces Club in London. It was tucked discretely away in a white stucco Georgian street. The high-gloss paneled door with buffed brass fittings looked like many others in the Mayfair. The usual understated polished nameplate was missing.

The club was open exclusively to those from the UK's Special Forces and its intelligence elite. Inside, it was a typical London club. There were green leather Winchester sofas, high backed chairs, paper racks, a dark wooden bar with shelves of single malt whisky and lots of oak panels.

Discrete waiters served tea or drinks in the members' lounge. Each had held the rank of senior warrant officer in the elite forces of the Army or the Marines. All were heavily vetted for security.

The dining room gleamed with polished silverware. Starched white table linen dazzled.

Harris looked old and tired. Roberts had thick-lensed glasses. Otherwise they might both have been cut from the same discrete grey cloth. Harris spoke softly, so as not to be overheard, as he tucked into his roast lamb.

Perfectly pink inside, it was served with mint sauce, brown gravy, carrots and boiled potatoes. Harris chewed appreciatively. He protested between mouthfuls.

"Look Roberts old chap; I don't see what this has to do with MI6. We're only responsible for foreign operations. This is clearly domestic. It's entirely in your bailiwick."

"Come on Harris. Don't be like that. We've helped you out often enough. You'll be retiring soon. Just do me one last favor. All I want is a way to check out what he's up to. You handled him before. You must be able to think of something. The man's so careful about what he says and does, especially on the phone. We need a break. The Home Secretary wants results."

"Does the PM know? She has a soft spot for Alex you know. So do I, if it comes to that. He did a bloody good job in Argentina. Ruffled a few feathers of course."

"No, Maggie's completely in the dark. There are plots within the cabinet to replace her. Getting too full of herself. Bossy. Not sticking to the protocols. Can't have that. Besides, we need to keep in with both sides. Same as always."

"Yes, you're right about that. Look, we have an agent, Maria Ramirez. She had a bit of a fling with him on their last caper In Argentina. She's really good. Ruthless. I'll transfer her to MI5 for a few weeks. See what happens."

* * *

Becky propelled Alex out of her bed with a push from a strong leg.

"Come on you, let's go grab some breakfast and chat things over."

He showered, whilst she was doing her auburn hair. It was darker than the ginger bush of her pubis.

Later, the two of them sat in a nearby greasy spoon. The cafe's tables were barely wiped Formica. Badly cleaned windows looked out onto passing Londoners rushing to the nearby underground station. Early morning workers were reading the Daily Mirror or the Sun over their egg and bacon rolls with brown sauce. An old tramp wrapped his hands around his cup of tea to suck the last warmth from it into his cold fingers.

A heavily tattooed, bleached blond and bleary-eyed waitress cheerily slapped their plates down.

"Ere y'are, two full English. That'll keep yer goin."

They gorged on the classic plebeian breakfast: bacon, two fried eggs, sausage dripping with fat, fried bread and black pudding. This was all washed down with strong sweet tea with milk. It was a heart attack on a plate. Becky slathered her food with tomato ketchup. He preferred Daddies, a piquant brown sauce. She waved an eggy fork at him.

"The miners and the electricity unions need to act together. The two industries are totally linked. Without coal, there's no power. Either union can bring the country to a halt. Together they're unbeatable."

"Just because you work for the Trades Union Congress, Becky, doesn't mean you can't see what that would do. The British coal industry can't compete with cheap coal from strip mines in Australia, South Africa and the US.

A strike like this only prolongs the agony. Think of how many ordinary people would suffer from this. Think of the damage to the economy."

"Come on Alex. You talk like a Tory. If the unions hadn't fought the bosses every step, we'd still have kids down in the mines and no worker protection at all."

He could see this was not going anywhere. Reluctantly, he broke contact from her mesmerizing green eyes.

"Sorry Becky, I've got to dash. Important meeting. Tonight, it's my place then."

"Fine, but I'm not letting you off the hook on this. It's to be continued."

He rode in the fusty warmth of a crowded tube train. He emerged from the underground station. It was just a short walk to the grey stone National Coal Board offices.

Becky caught the double-decker red bus to Trades Union House. She worked in public relations. Both thought of their desire to keep the relationship going. Each recognized that conflict over unfolding events was inevitable. It might drive them apart.

* * *

At the state owned National Coal Board headquarters, Sir Ian Macgregor sat across a meeting room table from Alex. Like the coal industry itself, the offices had seen better days. The oil portraits of past chairmen needed cleaning. Tobacco smoke had stained the ceilings. The overall impression was dull, dark and depressing.

Margaret Thatcher had called Sir Ian in to restructure and drastically downsize the coal industry. He was already famous and much hated for doing exactly that at British Steel. She really appreciated his no-nonsense style. He brought back restructuring expertise from his time in the US.

The deep-hewn coal from the many mines around the UK had served Britain well during the Industrial Revolution and on through WORLD WARII. Mostly, it was no longer competitive. Some mines were played out. In others, the costs were huge, compared with to those of strip-mined coal, easier to access from abroad. 100,000 ton bulk carriers and Britain's many ports made it a cheaper and a more reliable proposition.

The larger problem was the miners themselves. Alex knew that no mother wanted a son to delve into the choking blackness in the depths of the earth. It was dangerous, dirty, rough and unhealthy work. Despite this, mining villagers were fused into a tough and implacable force. Years of hardship, pit disasters and suffering together in close proximity made them stubborn and always ready to fight the bosses.

The miners' unions were the most militant of all, with the possible exception of the dockers. The dockers and the railway workers were essential to bring imported coal ashore and deliver it to where it was burnt. Sir Ian was determined to beat them all into submission. The government expected civil unrest and conflict.

Ian Macgregor was reviewing the situation in his office with Alex.

"This industry is going to be right-sized, whatever it takes! It'll mean taking on the miners, the dockers, the railway men and the electricity workers. Maybe the whole trade union movement will become embroiled if they call a general strike.

"How are our contingency plans going Alex?"

Alex handed Sir Ian a folder marked "Top Secret Copy No 1"

"Here, this shows how we've built up coal stocks at the power plants. Army drivers are being trained for further deliveries. In a few weeks, we'll be ready."

"We may not have a few weeks. What else have you got?"

Alex pushed across a second file.

"These are the plans to drastically reduce coal usage. There will be a three-day working week. There'll need to be political action to stop a general strike. We'll need a state of emergency."

"Don't worry about that. The Prime Minister is introducing legislation to stop strikes in sympathy and much else."

"If it's all right with you, Sir Ian, I'd like to go and see how things are on the ground?"

Sir Ian gave him a quizzical look.

"All right, but be careful. We don't want to provoke any incidents. I'll need you back here by Friday. Make sure we know where we can find you in a hurry."

* * *

"Becky was riding Alex hard, as they both came for the second time. She screamed her ecstasy, tossing her head. She was a Judo adept. *That explained her muscular suppleness.* The downside was that she pinned him to the bed, with a lock on each wrist. He thought, *Well it's not all bad.* He chided her.

"Hush love, the neighbors might complain."

She smirked at him, scooped her panties off the floor, hurling them at his head, then strutted into the bathroom. There was a piercing shriek.

He rushed in. She stood dripping on the floor-tiles, crushing herself against the far wall. She pointed speechlessly at the shower curtain. He did not know what to expect. He tore it open and stood well back. A small black beetle was slowly making its way towards the shower fitting.

Alex looked in disbelief. He shuddered, as if getting control of himself. Then he burst out laughing.

Becky screamed at him and started hitting him.

"Come on! Quick! Kill it!"

Alex cupped his hands, carefully scooping and cradling the wee beastie. Then, he shoved open the window with an elbow, releasing it outside.

"He's harmless. He's only got a short life. Who are we t' end it?"

She looked at him, astonished. No one she knew cared about insects. Then his hands started trembling. His jaw clamped tight. Beads of sweat appeared on his forehead. He staggered against the door jam.

"What on earth is it Alex? Tell me. Speak."

She could not get an answer from him. Maybe it was something to do with his nightmares?

* * *

The next week, sipping a breakfast orange juice in his apartment, he casually murmured,

"I'm going away for a few days. I want t'see what the mood's like in the pit towns."

She exploded.

"For God's sake man, don't you even read the papers? They're preparing for war."

"Yes, I know what your agitating union leaders are saying. My experience is you can't beat finding out what's going at the lowest level."

She bashed him with the newspaper in frustration.

"Go on then, but you'll find these strikes'll be a hundred per cent solid."

* * *

The man in jeans and a laborer's jacket sat sipping his tea on the 8:00 am train from London to Glasgow. The second-class carriages were dingy and tired. It was another state-owned industry that needed reform and massive investment. He poked at his British Rail pork pie with some disgust. He remembered the old joke, "The wrappers contain the following instruction. 'We know this tastes like crap, but don't throw out of the window. It might derail the down train.'"

Three other men squeezed into the empty seats around him. Others dropped into theirs across the aisle. The newcomers turned out to be electricity union delegates. From their chatter, they had been attending a meeting with other unions in London.

Alex pulled the Daily Mirror up to mask his face. The headlines were all about the political crisis. The text was generally supporting the workers.

He listened to them intently.

"Well, if we come out with the miners, it looks like we could be breaking the law."

"Bloody 'ell Harry! We've got to do what's right. Bugger the law! Solidarity that's what we need. If we all act together, nothing can stop us."

A calmer voice interjected.

"Steady on now, Bill. If we break the law, the courts'll take away our funds. Then what? Besides, I'm not sure all my members'll come out. They've families t' support."

Alex folded his newspaper and headed for the buffet car. Another person in a trench coat, who had been pretending to sleep, followed him from the back of the carriage. He kept at a distance.

Sipping from his bottle of Newcastle Brown, Alex eavesdropped on the buffet car's passengers. They stood enjoying their drinks, but probably not enjoying their plastic looking Kraft cheese sandwiches.

The coming showdown between government and unions was the topic of the day. Many were frightened for their own jobs, if the miners and electricity workers came out. One woman, with an Aberdeen accent, put it bluntly,

"It's a' very well for ye to talk aboot the Government beein' thrown out. 'Ave got three wee bairns to feed and rent t' pay."

* * *

Later that evening Alex checked into a working-man's bed and breakfast, close to Polmaise colliery in Stirling-shire. He knew that the mine was slated for closure. Geological faults meant it was completely unviable. It was a clear-cut case.

Next morning "Red" Mick McGahey the fiery and volatile leader of the Scottish miners' union was due to speak to the workforce. He was a long-time member of the Communist party and a local hero. It was he that had negotiated the provision of pithead baths and laundry services for the miners.

Alex listened to the chatter in the taproom of the nearest pub. It was packed. Tobacco smoke swirled around. Beer mats advertising local brews were scattered across the iron-legged tables. Personal pewter tankards hung from hooks above the bar. Others were gripped in the scarred and battered hands of local miners.

The bar staff was kept busy, surrounded by thirsty miners clamoring to be served. They pulled foaming pints with practiced ease. Two tugs from the long wood handle of a beer tap almost filled a glass. Each handle had a badge showing its contents. As the foam subsided, the pints were topped off. The canny miners demanded full measure.

Alex was enjoying a pint of "heavy." Scottish beer was unavailable in London. A weasel-like man watched him furtively from the other side of the room. His beady eyes stared stealthily from the shadows behind a pillar.

A union official handed out leaflets. He gave Alex, a stranger, a suspicious glance. When Alex spoke with a Gorbles accent, he moved on, reassured.

"Thanks brother."

Alex listened to several miners saying they knew the colliery was doomed. There was palpable fear. There was also elation at the collective strength of the men, their union and their community.

"Aye. Am no sayin' we should na strike. Am no a scab."

To some surprise around 8:00 pm, Mick McGahey walked into the pub. Excitedly, his union members crowded round him.

"Will ye have a drink Michael?"

"A wee Bells."

"Anythin' in it?"

"Another wee Bells."

* * *

In a windowless meeting room in MI5, Dr. Maria Ramirez stood ready to give her report to Roberts. She was not asked to sit. There was the usual green baize-clothed table. A flask of water and four upside-down tumblers stood in its center. Roberts poured himself a glass, without offering her one. Her polished agate eyes masked her fury.

"Get on with it then woman!"

"Sir Ian Macgregor seems very pleased with his work, as far as we can tell.

"There are two points of concern. He's having an affair with Rebecca Hardcastle."

She pushed a file across to him.

Her new boss, flipped through it, pausing occasionally, as something caught his attention.

"Hmm, she has a first in Sociology from the LSE. Oh, Oh! She went to Moscow three times in the last four years. Supposedly it was official trade union business. That's a real worry. What else?"

"Alex McDonald traveled incognito up to Scotland. He's been mixing with the likes of Mick McGahey and several other activists and Communists. He could be their mole in Sir Ian's camp."

"What do you advise?"

"We need to tap the subject's phones and apartment. We should have him tailed around the clock. Maybe I need to get back in touch with him."

Roberts wanted to take things more slowly.

"Let's set the bugs and the surveillance, but hold off on the last point for now. He seems to be well in with both Sir Ian and the Prime Minister. We don't want this to blow up in our faces. Give him enough rope and he might hang himself."

Seething, Ramirez gave the required "Yes sir." She remembered how Alex had stolen her prize operation in Argentina. It left her in a very embarrassing and quite dangerous situation in Buenos Aires. He had not even tried to get in touch with her afterwards. *I'm going to get that bastard.*

CHAPTER FOUR

Picket Line

COAL NOT DOLE

SHEFFIELD TRADES COUNCIL SAYS

SUPPORT THE MINERS

IT'S NOT JUST MINERS' JOBS
THEY ARE FIGHTING FOR

UNITY WILL WIN

SCABS WILL LOSE

THATCHER PAYS THE COPS

TO STARVE KIDS

Placards and banners waved on the Yorkshire miners picket lines. Alex had changed his clothes to a smart suit. He was reviewing the crisis with the managers at the Maltby Colliery in South Yorkshire. The dirty run-down colliery and its spoil heaps were a blot on the landscape. The coal-loading yard on the railway slashed a blackened wound into the town.

Unusually, the tall brick chimney of the power plant was not belching black smoke. The aged steel winding tower had enormous spinning wheels. Their steel cables for dropping the miner's cages deep into the black void of the main shaft stood eerily silent. Today, the darkest depths of the earth would not swallow its tightly packed cluster of rugged bantering men.

The grimy windows of the colliery meeting room reverberated with the noise from outside. The striking miners and their pickets had the raucous support of their brass band. The bass notes of the sousaphone beat out the time for the rhythmic chanting.

"Maggie, Maggie, Maggie! Out! Out! Out!"

"The Miners—united—will never be defeated."

And as some workers tried to enter the compound,

"Scabs! Scabs! Scabs!"

Within, the dingy office building, a rattled manager was struggling to be heard over the din. Yellow strip lights shone on his colleagues in their off-the-peg clothes. Alex's Savile Row suit, complete with silk pocket-handkerchief and white cuffs showing, stood out like a sore thumb. Mentally, he noted the need to dress down for such meetings. He hated to embarrass these good people.

"Well Mr. McDonald, yer can 'ear the row outside. This pit's bin 'ere sin 1910. 'Ow d'yer expect 'em to feel? Ow'd yer think we feel? There'll be no jobs round 'ere when you close the pit."

Later, Alex said his goodbyes with handshakes. Then he made some notes in an adjacent office. Finally, in the dusty yard, the driver held the door open for him to enter the British Coal car.

The movement was spotted through the wrought iron gates to screams and a rushing forward by the mob. The police pushed back the picket line, so the car could leave.

Then the cops gave way under the pressure. One had his helmet knocked off. They still wore the old and unsuitable high, black bobbies' helmets with enormous shiny badges. Alex had grabbed one for a drunken dare when a student at Glasgow University.

Cobbled stones flew overhead. Angry shouts and placards, used as weapons, did the rest.

In the back seat of the roomy black car, Alex looked out with mounting concern. *This is getting nasty.* A heavy pole was denting the roof. The vehicle began rocking alarmingly. He sat up. The window next to him was smashed with a brick. It showered his pin-striped suit with glass. A grasping hand clawed at him through the window. A face flushed with anger yelled, "Get 'im out lads." Others bellowed "Scab!"

Instinct took over. He drove an elbow down into the reaching arm. There was a snap. The man screamed. The limb was withdrawn.

Alex slid across the leather seat, shouting to the driver.

"Come on Jack! Out the other side. We've got to get back to the police line."

He slid across the back seat. Then he smashed the other door into a smaller cluster of pickets. The group staggered back, shouting. He dragged the cowering driver with him.

There were camera flashes all round, as he fought his way through. He broke the nose of one man. Finally, the police enfolded them both in a protective circle. The cops dragged them back inside the gates. Alex's cheek smarted. A blow from a stick had slashed it open.

The driver slumped, seated on the ground. One mine official held him up. Another bandaged his bloody head wound.

* * *

That night Alex was back in his London flat. A helicopter had lifted them to safety. The whine of its turbine and clattering rotor had drowned out the pickets' fury.

He grasped a half tumbler of Scotch, as he relived breaking the picket's arm.

"Why can't I control myself Becky?"

Gloomily, Becky looked at the swelling bruise around the stitches in his cheek.

"You had cause love, but you shouldn't have been there."

She clicked on the TV. It was the news. The segment opened on a row of sooty miners' cottages. A long shot showed the idyllic, green Yorkshire countryside. Then the camera zoomed in on the Dickensian dullness around the pit gates.

They focused on the agonized face of the man with the broken arm. Blood spattered another's face. Paramedics were loading them both into an ambulance. A still and very clear picture of Alex punching the second man followed. Becky winced.

"Bloody hell Alex. This is bad."

He took a deep swallow from his glass.

"Tell me aboot it. I swear I was jis tryin' to get oot o there."

An enraged union spokesman bawled at the interviewer, waving his arms.

"This is 'ow the bosses treat a peaceful demonstration. We'll not put up wi' this! You'll see."

Angry pickets brandished their fists behind him. They roared their support. Some fierce looking women waved rolling pins and other domestic weapons.

Alex took another gulp of whisky. He poured some more.

"Oh shit!"

* * *

In 10 Downing Street, Prime Minister Thatcher was watching the same program. Her private sitting room was part of the family apartment, hidden above the splendor of the meeting and Cabinet rooms.

Her husband, multi-millionaire businessman, Dennis Thatcher, raised his fifth gin and tonic as Alex appeared on the screen.

"Here's to you sir!"

He was much older than his wife. He possessed a shrewd business brain. It had helped him build a successful paint business. Added to this, his political connections made him a valued non-executive director. One, otherwise "dry" US company even installed a bar in its UK Boardroom, to recruit him.

The PM smiled indulgently at Dennis. He had always encouraged her and funded her meteoric rise to Prime Minister. Now he was amiable and a bit of an old soak. He kept out of politics, at least in public. She remarked,

"Mmm. That's Alex McDonald. He's a hero, but we can't say so. It was all hush hush. We'll need to get him out of the Coal Board soon. He certainly surfaces where the action is."

"Have another snifter dear."

"No thank you Dennis. I've work to do tonight."

"I wonder where we can use that young man again. If only we had a thousand like him."

She changed the subject,

"I hear some of party grandees are out to get me Dennis."

"Nonsense dear. You'll eat 'em all for breakfast."

* * *

Next morning, the PM rose at her customary 4:30 am. She was reading the early editions in her study under a green-shaded brass table lamp.

"EX-COMMANDO THUG BEATS UP STRIKERS"

"…Royal Marine Major Alex McDonald now works for Kendrick & Company, Thatcher's favorite consulting firm….

Why do they get so much government work without competitive tender…?

What was he doing in Maltby…? The people have the right t' know…!"

She thought, *Rivals in Alex's firm must have leaked information.*

Irritated, the Prime Minister tapped her pencil against her teeth.

* * *

Summoned to a meeting in Whitehall, Alex faced a somewhat oily civil servant and his silent colleague. As usual, the venue was spartan and windowless. He assumed these were MI5 operatives. They had that look.

"This meeting is off the record. Understood?"

"Fine, but what do you want? I'm likely to be reassigned as a result of the Maltby fiasco."

"Do you have any idea who gave my name to the press?"

"Never mind that. We want to ask you about the activities of Rebecca Halstead. We think she works for the Soviets"

Alex snorted indignantly.

"You don't know what you're talking about!"

He stood up and walked purposefully toward the door.

"Sorry gentlemen. I won't do this. Besides, she is not keen to see me anymore."

After he had left, the silent man scribbled a note on a report,

"Refused to cooperate…Highly suspicious behavior …Not to be trusted."

* * *

Back in his flat, Becky had left a phone message.

"Look, when you come to your senses, give up that stupid job and join the right side. Then, maybe we can meet again."

Disconsolate, he slumped in an armchair. *I am on the wrong side. I need to get out of this mess.* He'd miss Becky. He needed her arms around him more than ever. Maybe he could win her back. *How?*

He steeled himself. Reaching out, he deleted her message and poured himself a stiff drink. *Oh well, what new excitement will tomorrow bring?*

CHAPTER FIVE

Showdown at Kendrick

"Allow yourself to think only those thoughts that match your principles and can bear the light of day. Your daily choices, your thoughts and your actions fashion the person you become. Your integrity determines your destiny."

Heraclitus

The twelve Kendrick European directors sat poker-faced. They smiled falsely at each other around the London Board table. The highly-polished mahogany reflected the discrete lighting. Each brain whirred with calculations as to how to seek personal advantage. Notepads lay untouched on the leather blotters in front of them. One or two had casually left discretely expensive pens in front of them, Mont Blanc, Caran d'Ache, Cartier and Graf Von Faber-Castel.

The head of Europe was haranguing Alex. His immaculate pin-striped suit was even more perfect than the others around the room. It was double breasted. His broad silk tie, dark blue with white polka dots, matched the handkerchief in his top pocket. He felt it added a sense of creativity to that of power and credibility. He looked over his half spectacles at Alex.

"Look, we don't know who leaked your information to the papers. There is no evidence whatsoever that it came from here. Be reasonable. Why would we highlight the non-competitive contracts we receive?"

Alex glanced bleakly from face to face. One of his British co-directors was looking rather smug and began doodling on his pad. *A sign of nerves. I bet it was you. Ye bawbag!* It was Algy Smythe. Alex nicknamed him "Hatchet-man." He was a thoroughly nasty character, only happy when his clients laid off thousands to meet his cost-cutting recommendations. He actually kept score of how many jobs he had cut each year. The running total ran into hundreds of thousands.

Alex looked at several of the other directors in silence. As intended, this built an eagerness for his response.

"Well then, Chairman and colleagues, I thank you for your time."

An additional pause escalated the tension. He noted the fleeting smirk hovering around the thin lips of the doodling Hatchet-man. *Someone'll get you one day, pal.*

"It is only fair to tell you that I've decided to leave the firm over this. We cannot function without mutual trust."

Suddenly all the directors sat forward. Alex's connection to the UK Prime Minister was the source of huge prestige in government circles. It spilled over into lucrative opportunities from other governments around the world. There was a list of privatizations coming. Each would be worth tens of millions in fees.

The Chairman flushed and took off the intimidating glasses. He mopped his brow with his spotted handkerchief. His tone became unctuous and conciliatory.

"Now, let's not be hasty Alex. I am certain we can reassure you about all this. Besides, we've never had a director leave voluntarily, other than for retirement. Our work is far too lucrative and interesting for that."

Alex arose. Either side of him, concerned directors pushed back their chairs to observe his response. Others leaned forward to listen. This discussion led directly to the value of the firm. Their own personal cash flows were in the balance. The mansions in the stock-broker belt, the sailing yachts, the villas in Tuscany, their children's places at Eton and Oxford, all were at risk.

"We can discuss the details later. My mind's made up. In confidence, I want to share something with you. It'll help you understand my position.

"Two weeks ago, the representative of a cabinet minister approached me. He showed me a file alleging that Colonel Gadhafi, the Libyan dictator, is funding the strikers.

"The problem is that I have other information showing this to be a fabrication. The facts have been twisted. False ones added."

A couple of weeks earlier he had confronted Becky with this accusation. In response, she had shared confidential papers about the union's Libyan connection. They comprehensively refuted the Government version.

"Neither this firm nor I can be associated with this and other dirty tactics being deployed to beat the strikers."

No longer smug, Hatchet-man raised his palms in disbelief. He looked around the table. His eyes pleaded for support.

"That's just politics. Much worse happens all around the world. It has nothing to do with us. Besides, I thought you had great respect for Sir Ian."

"I do. He's an extremely righteous Presbyterian. He'd have no truck with mud-slinging. That's why they wanted me to push the story. I approached the Prime Minister's Private Secretary to protest. He told me she was aware of it and that the matter was decided.

"Sorry gentlemen and lady. I'm determined. I'm sure the UK government will continue to pass contracts to you. I'll be in tomorrow to make financial arrangements."

With that, Alex calmly left the room. The meeting went on for hours thereafter.

* * *

He hailed a black London taxi. Settling into the back seat, he punched Becky's office number into his mobile phone. She was out. He left her a brief message.

"OK. I've quit. I need to see you."

Back at home, he shucked off his work clothes. He donned his comfortable Wranglers and a Black Sabbath T-shirt. Putting his feet on the smoked glass coffee table, he stretched out to think.

He would have to speak to Sir Ian at the National Coal Board. *That should go all right. He's a strong character and not dependent on me.*

Financially, I'll be very well off, especially given my modest lifestyle. My shares in the firm are worth at least $15 million. The question is what should I do next?

The white phone on a side table trilled. He snatched at it, almost dropping it. *These tangly coils drive me nuts! It must be Becky.*

It was his mentor, the former Colonel and current Human Resources Director of Kendrick. Alex released a breath of disappointment.

"Well, you certainly set the cat amongst the pigeons here Alex. Some directors wanted to fudge your stock value, till I pointed out that you could still do them great harm."

"That doesn't surprise me, the miserable bastards. Thanks for your support."

"Don't mention it. Anyway, I called with your next opportunity."

"Hey, maybe I need a few weeks break."

"Nonsense, Action Man. Besides, my friend at Gold-ring Silverblatt telephoned. They'd heard something. Seen the newspapers and TV of course. I put 'em straight. Just pick up the phone when they ring. They have something right up your street. It won't clash with your refined sense of ethics either."

"Thanks, I'll think about it."

"Well don't think too long. We can talk more tomorrow. You'll be in to clear your office and agree separation terms. That was the other purpose of my call. Is 10:00 am OK?"

Afterwards, Alex stared at the phone. It lay annoyingly inert. Becky did not call.

* * *

At MI5 Roberts and his team were chewing over reports on Alex leaving Kendrick. Through his thick lenses, he appraised Ramirez with a critical look. In the time on Harris's team, she had completed a number of outstanding assignments. *No other operative was as effective in making troublesome people disappear without trace. That could be useful.*

He slitted his eyes. *Thickened out a bit during her time in the service. A few crow's feet too. Still not bad looking. I like 'em ripe.* Licking his lips, he pushed his copy of the McDonald file aside.

"What do you say Ramirez? You know him best."

"He's a loose cannon out there. He refused to cooperate on the Gadhafi thing. Our source at Kendrick claims he might well leak secret material from that fiasco. He's back with his commie girlfriend. Now, he's to be involved with highly sensitive matters in Eastern Europe. He needs to be dealt with—permanently. Just say the word, sir."

"Sorry, can't do that. Maggie still keeps an eye on him. She approves of his new role, 'Sorting out decades of failed socialism,' she called it."

"Sir Ian gave him an outstanding reference to Goldring. You've seen the copy. Macgregor's the sort that doesn't write things he doesn't believe to be true. Our other friend at Kendrick, the Colonel, vouches for him too. He's a wily bird. I back his judgment.

"We'll keep him under grade 2 surveillance over in the UK. We'll ask MI6 to watch what he's up to in Europe. If he really is working for the Ruskies, things are too sensitive to let him loose on their former satellite states.

"All OK?"

Ramirez hid the black anger gnawing at her entrails. *I'll get him, if it's the last thing I do.*

"Yes sir!"

"Jump to it then."

* * *

A week earlier Alex flew into New York on the Concord. One of Goldring Silverblatt's corporate helicopters whisked him away. It landed on the roof of the Goldring Tower. Determined not to be, he was impressed. They had way more style than Kendrick.

They sat in an opulent meeting room. Paintings of confident past chairmen hung around the walls. There was green silk wallpaper and polished hardwood panels with matching fittings. The table had a reflective waxed sheen.

The Chairman and Chief Executive of Goldring Silverblatt, Ted Barger was making his pitch to Alex over their vodka martinis. He was immaculately dressed in a dark blue Italian suit. *Looks like it cost $10,000.* His hand-tailored, striped shirt had a white button-down collar. Barger's reputation was brash and pushy. Time magazine had featured him as a contender for "most influential man in the world" a year earlier. Alex could tell that he was in selling mode. Barger had softened his style.

"We have the greatest respect for Kendrick. As you know, we are working jointly with them on several privatizations in the UK and elsewhere. We know you were instrumental in winning much of that for them."

Barger puffed himself up slightly,

"Goldring is always invited in as a matter of course. Our fees are multiples of those Kendrick gets."

Alex raised an eyebrow. He knew that Goldring deployed its enormous financial market power as lead underwriter on some of the privatizations. It was the top-rated investment bank in London, New York and Hong Kong. Spreading new branches in Asia and the newly free Eastern Europe gave them unmatched global reach. The top rating applied to mergers and acquisitions, privatizations, IPOs and the bond markets. Additionally, Goldring hired ex-members of the US administration. In turn, its senior people often took top jobs in government, especially in the US Treasury.

Alex was about to protest that Goldring received more because they took higher risks. The CEO smiled and raised his glass, as if in a toast.

"I've read some of your articles in the business press, Alex. They're excellent PR for your firm. It's clear that you love high-level strategy. Well, whatever the strategy, it needs to be measured against the resulting financial value of the business in question. The financial structure and funding of the firm are another crucial element. We do all that. Additionally, we execute, through divestitures, acquisitions, spin-offs and much more. Kendrick can only suggest these things. We make mega bucks every step of the way. We create corporations, tear them apart or bury them. Whether clients win or lose, we make money."

Ruefully, Alex recollected the occasions when a firm he was advising, was suddenly acquired or dismembered by investment banks like Goldring. There were other cases when his place at the right hand of an important Chairman had been usurped by Goldring. They could get the job done. *The man's right. They operate at a higher level of strategy. They make big bets. I'd love to play at the top table.*

* * *

Becky cuddled close to Alex on her couch. He was explaining the new job. She was more than skeptical. He slanted his description in terms that might appeal to her.

"I'll be helping the newly liberated peoples of the old Soviet empire. Now that the Berlin Wall's down and the Czechs and the rest are shaking themselves free, the old regimes have set up massive industrial "combinats." They make no sense in an open market. They receive quotas of inputs. They measure output in weight rather than value. That's nuts. They waste labor. They're all run down. The machinery and product designs are Stalin era. They need sorting out before these countries can rise from their knees."

Sitting up sharply, she whacked his head with a copy of the Economist.

"Listen to Mister Bloated Capitalist. You'll carve up the pie and hand it to the rapacious western companies. There'll be mass unemployment. Seventy years of socialist sweat and blood'll be down the toilet."

They argued for hours. Both knew that the other was partly right. She smiled at him. *I love this hulking hard man, with his soft spot for insects and fascinating discussions about world affairs. He treats me as an equal. At least he wanted me to agree before he took the job. The sad part is he'll be away a lot.*

* * *

She looked at him sleeping. She gently traced the new scar on his face. *Our relationship's so volatile. At least his screaming nightmares are fewer. Caressing his forehead always calms him. Still, I wish he'd share more with me. He sometimes babbles in Spanish in his dreams. That and his scars likely mean he was a prisoner during the Falklands war.*

She'd tried to raise that insight with him. He gave the usual reply with a forced smile.

"I'd love to tell you darling, but I'd have to kill you. It would be a pity. I've got used to having you around."

So, he still mistrusted her. It hurt. Later, she checked the newspaper files in the library. The microfiches showed pictures of downcast marines, with drooping shoulders. The Governor had ordered them to surrender at Port Stanley, after a brief firefight with the Argentine invaders. Alex was not in any of them. *What then?*

Oblivious to this, Alex focused on his new job. He knew the theory of his new role. He could hardly wait to see what things were really like as a top banker.

CHAPTER SIX

All is Politics

Politics have no relation to morality

Machiavelli

Alex's plane landed with a gentle bump and a squeak of tires. In 1991, Poland's Lublin airport was bleak. It doubled as a fighter base. A line of grounded, dusty MIG 21D fighters languished at the far side of the runway. A four-jet, grey USAF Starlifter was loading some big crates. *Wonder what's in those?*

In the dull concrete bleakness of the terminal, sad kiosks sold grungy Polish brands of cigarettes, snacks, sweets and the newspapers. Fortunately, the Goldring team was whisked through the VIP line at customs and immigration. They bypassed all the endless queues. The culture of communist officialdom still lingered. As before, the elites avoided the boring difficulties of the masses.

On the drive into town, Alex noted that the concrete road was wide enough to accommodate four tanks abreast. There was a Soviet war memorial. Its bronze statues were frozen in heroic poses. *Will Poles ever feel secure enough to tear those down? The big bear still lurks on the border.*

He was amazed at how much of Poland remained agricultural and backward. On the farms off the road he glimpsed horses pulling both ploughs and carts.

Cars were few and mainly rickety Polish built Ladas. A sprinkling of other obsolete makes from former COMECON countries rattled along amongst them. Officials still favored massive black Zil limousines. These looked like throwbacks to the late 50s.

He observed that the first Mercedes and BMWs were beginning to appear. *Foreigners? Gangsters? Oligarchs? Maybe all of these? And of course, our own Goldring Mercedes 600 limo.*

Many of his colleagues from Goldring were Germans. One confided in him.

"In 1945 Poland stole large parts of eastern Germany. The Russians seized parts of Poland. My family owned estates in East Prussia. Now the place is ruined. Germany has the expertise and the capital. We will run Poland, as was always intended."

Alex moved a little away from the man, while commenting,

"Well there are still strong feelings here. People have memories of mass murder, rape and ethnic cleansing; handed down from their parents and grandparents. I'd keep your views to yourself and a low profile if I were you."

Alex recalled the industries his teams on the ground were already involved in: steel, shipbuilding in Gdansk, and car assembly. *All are like something from the Industrial Revolution. Wall-eyed, alcohol-soused workers, dark satanic mills, grime and pollution. Their only future is extinction or foreign takeover.*

The hotel was typical of those in which the apparatchiks and party members had stayed. It was better than the hotels for the ordinary people, but absolutely bloody awful. A sign at reception read "We charge $50 to turn on the fax machine."

His bathroom faucet spewed coal dust along with the brownish water. Inadequately thin curtains did not meet in the center of the windows. He looked out through a grimy pane on rows of badly built apartment blocks. The driving rain did little to lighten the gloomy scene.

* * *

The Poles he dealt with certainly liked their vodka. He was in a mid-morning meeting in Lublin. His head still spun from the previous evening.

The various interested parties in the biggest export earner, the copper and silver mining business, were each pushing their own agendas. Mostly this happened behind the scenes. He'd heard that enormous bribes and fulsome promises were commonplace. The scramble to steal the big industries was on.

Meanwhile, western multinationals circled the chaos like hungry vultures, ready to swoop in at the right moment. Goldring knew them all. Nothing happened without the bank's connivance and profit. It feels great to be a power-broker. *But how do I make sure we do the right thing at the same time? Can I?*

While the interpreters translated, and mangled the speakers' words, Alex wrestled with the issues. *Who owns the mines? The national government assumes it does. They need the income to fund their schemes and plans.*

The workers feel they're entitled to ownership. They've slaved in the mines. Parents or siblings likely died in them. The old Marxist mantra, "Workers' ownership of the means of production." was drilled into them at school. Now, they forget the abject failure of the old order.

Regional and city governments see remote Warsaw politicians as carpetbaggers. They want local control and any profits to fund their own political power and projects.

Lastly, the wily and rapacious managers are maneuvering behind the scenes. The businesses organization is in a terrible mess, but they're seeking to channel as much as possible into their own pockets. They've mastered capitalism bloody fast. Most switched seamlessly from the old ways to the new. Elites are hardy. They stay in the saddle under communism or capitalism.

* * *

After several such assignments, Alex was becoming a master of the process. He described it to Becky on an increasingly rare weekend in London.

"First there's a pretty brutal chopping up of the whole mess into manageable chunks. Most of the combinats are vertically and horizontally integrated."

"OK, cut the jargon or you'll be eating alone."

"Right, each combinat owns all sorts of businesses, hence the name. The business units are more or less related to the core activity. In a centrally planned system, it was the only way they could rely on the linkages working. They needed to ensure they got the raw materials and machinery necessary to make their products and to sustain their workforces.

"The Czech engineering group I worked on near Prague was a great example. It had a steel works. To make the steel, they needed iron-ore mines, coalmines and power stations. So, they owned those. The workers wanted holidays, so they operated resort hotels. Consumer goods were hard to get in the communist system, so they ran shops to sell the people TVs and everything else. Senior managers had nice little love nests, provided by the firm.

"I already told you how one Chief Executive of a construction company took a shine to one of our young MBAs. He offered to build her a house so they could get together. We had to get her out of there.

"No one knew how much anything cost or which business units were viable. The whole thing became a shambles."

Increasingly frustrated, Becky broke in.

"Some of their old ways sound very sensible. They ensured local employment. Most of the profits stayed in the business. The workers had holidays too. What's wrong with that?"

"Well sorry to disabuse you, it isn't sensible. There were no profits and the businesses only existed due to state subsidies and government contracts. That truck manufacturer I visited in Slovenia sold all its output to the army and the former Yugoslav government. The vehicles were thirty years out of date. They had no chance of meeting international emission standards. Nobody wants them anymore."

He recounted his experiences at another truck and car manufacturer, Tatra, in Czechoslovakia.

"It's the second oldest vehicle producer in the world after Daimler Benz. I was only there because I was traveling with the team on that assignment. That team was in meetings. I was at a loose end. The gate-keeper, asked whether I'd like to see their museum. It was the most modern building in a crumbling collection of old factory buildings."

Becky was irritated. Her mother had been a staunch trade unionist and her grandmother a suffragette. She could hear her grandmother's voice.

Men always have good reasons why their ways are the best. Take no notice of them girl.

Oblivious to her mounting frustration, Alex smiled at her.

"The curator had little to do. He charged me the equivalent of ten cents. He had to scrabble around in his desk for the ticket roll. I must have been his first visitor for ages. He turned on the lights in the museum.

"The place was amazing. They have a dusty collection of mechanical marvels. One car, from the 30s, looked almost exactly like the Volkswagen Beetle. He told me that the Nazis stole both the air-cooled engine design and the basic shape. Of course, the Germans deny that.

"Tatra was a source of large and sophisticated communist limousines. They had a futuristic look. It also made army trucks for the whole Eastern Block. Other exhibits included a light aircraft and a large snowmobile. The sheer ingenuity and variety demonstrated advanced and creative engineering skills.

"I was really sad. Over a beer, our team told me there was no hope for the place. Foreigners would pick up the pieces either immediately or soon after mass privatization."

She finally flared up, eyes flashing and face flushing. She jabbed a finger toward him.

"How many of these stories are you going to tell me? Goldring and its clients are just looting the place! That means you buster!

"I want you to see what's going on in Russia. Let's have a holiday there."

Taken aback, he readily acquiesced.

* * *

In 1971, over twenty years earlier, Alex had taken a tourist trip to Moscow. He should have sought permission, but the Marines never questioned him about it. He assumed they were unaware. In those days, computer integration and electronic surveillance were still primitive.

He had been appalled. He shared his impressions with Becky as they discussed their planned visit.

"The border guards were really nasty. They wore military uniforms with high fronted peaked caps. They just tipped our suitcases out onto the dusty floor.

"We were herded everywhere. The guide was from Intourist, the state travel agency. She watched us like a hawk. Surly babushkas controlled every level in the ridiculously enormous Hotel Rossiya. It must have been a mile square. The food was beyond inedible. We tried to order drinks in the bar. The old crones in charge ignored everyone. They just chatted among themselves. They only had straight vodka, vodka with bison grass, vodka with ginger and several other vodkas in bilious colors.

"Soldiers in uniform rolled drunkenly around Red Square at ten in the morning. The streets were wide and empty. Only official cars sped by. Some had motorcycle outriders.

"Old women shoveled mountains of snow from the streets. It was -21C. If you took off yer hat, yer ears'd fall off. Outside all the shops, there were long, shuffling queues of heavily wrapped and grim-faced women. It was grey, nasty and bleak."

Becky was astonished. She fondly remembered her own prior visits. She pictured the welcoming faces of the friendly Russian trade unionists. The golden domes gleamed inside the impressive Kremlin walls. She recognized some of his description, but felt differently. She earnestly pleaded.

"Did nothing impress you?"

"Yes, the history for one. The endless cases displaying the Tsar's jewels and his enormous coach in the Kremlin Museum. You realize how desperately they needed a revolution. While the peasants grubbed for food the aristocrats were living in astonishing luxury.

"Out of town, each state's pavilion at the Museum of the Peoples was full of showpieces. We saw huge rockets. Their space capsules were tiny, cramped and crude compared to those of the US. They blasted them into space first though.

"The subway was modern and lavish. Its stations were in marble with chandeliers. Russian taste had a heavy, almost Victorian floridity. Every sixty seconds on the dot a train zoomed up.

"The people wore dowdy clothes, worn and many years out of date. They avoided talking to us. A couple of overly friendly "language students" tried to engage me in conversation. Annoyingly, there were no honey traps though."

She gave him a dig in the ribs.

"Ouch. Overall, it was a miserably grim place. I felt sorry for the Russians."

* * *

Two weeks later, he clasped her hand as they shuffled through the throng at immigration. Moscow airport was chaotic, but better than before. In 1992 Russia was in turmoil. He mused, ed muse*In a centrally controlled state, if you remove the center, collapse follows.*

He noticed many changes, mostly for the worse. Watery-eyed wizened pensioners wore rows of war medals on their tattered old coats. They hung around street corners. They were selling matches, single cigarettes or cheap Bic pens. Becky was incensed.

"See what your brave new world brings! These people stopped Hitler's tanks with their bare hands. Their families starved. Twenty million died for the motherland. They rebuilt their shattered nation. Now look."

"Well, there are more cars around and some people look quite prosperous. We dined in splendor in the Metropole hotel, serenaded by soulful singing and balalaika music. That particular dining room used to be reserved for the KGB. Now anyone can go."

"Anyone who can afford it you mean. The new elites, gangsters and oligarchs live well, but the masses are starving on the streets."

He sighed. *This trip's no going well.*

* * *

Over the next few weeks, Becky finally conceded that many of her cherished beliefs had proved false. Collectivization of farms, central planning and ignoring market economics had led to collapse. The interesting part was that in the UK her trade union bosses held firm to their previous views. They thought that new and better socialism was needed. Their concept included a return to widespread state ownership and high tariffs on imported goods to protect the workers' jobs. Strong government control and taxes on the bosses completed their vision. She reflected, *Alex thinks he can find a better way, but I seriously doubt it.*

* * *

Back in his apartment, Alex received a recorded delivery letter. It summoned him to a meeting in the same MI6 building he had visited before his Argentinean escapades. The signature was illegible. He was mildly curious. *Maybe it'll be a meeting with Harris? I'll hear him out. If they want to involve me in anything, the answer'll* be "No." *My undercover mission in Buenos Aires during the Falklands War nearly got me killed. Afterward they tried to screw me.*

CHAPTER SEVEN

Assassin Wanted

"Assassination is the extreme form of censorship."

George Bernard Shaw

"The best government is a tyranny, tempered by an occasional assassination."

Voltaire

Alex stepped from a taxi outside the MI6 building. Mounting the steps, he handed his letter of invitation and then his driving license to a leery, uniformed guard. The man consulted his list. He muttered into a telephone. Shortly, a severe looking woman with a thin line for a mouth led him through the corridors. She ushered him into yet another windowless meeting room. He winked at a camera watching him from a high corner.

Seconds later, three people marched in. Harris was not one of them. Alex was surprised.

Their leader had thick, black eyebrows, in contrast to his iron-grey hair. When he spoke, they waggled about, as though they had a life of their own. *They resemble demented beetles.* The man thrust out a hand. Smiling at his thought, Alex shook it.

"My name's Judd. I'm Harris's replacement. He retired last year. He spoke very highly of you."

"Well the feeling wasn't mutual. I'm finished with all that."

The three spooks glanced at each other looking pained. Alex studied them. *They must have a factory for cloning spies, iron-grey hair, medium height, lean, and utterly unmemorable. Maybe Judd got to the top simply due the eyebrows. They distinguished him from the crowd.*

Judd looked him in the eye and lightly touched his arm.

"Well let's sit down old man. Water?"

Alex accepted the proffered glass. Always suspicious, he waited till they sipped theirs before drinking.

"You're still covered by the official secrets act you know."

Alex raised his eyes to the ceiling.

"And?"

"What I'm about to share with you stays in this room."

"It always does."

"You've been doing good work, helping to sort out the former Soviet Empire. John Major's government is impressed by the reports they receive. Your piece in *The Independent Newspaper* on what was wrong and how to fix it caught his eye."

Alex remained tight-lipped at the blatant flattery. The article was a PR piece to polish Goldring's image. He remembered his last reception at 10 Downing Street. He had met the new Prime Minister and was less than impressed.

There had been the usual slow ascent up the staircase, as the queue of worthies waited to be announced. At each step, hung a portrait of a former Prime Minister. They were in ascending order from Sir Robert Walpole, the first, at the bottom. At the top of the stairs was the previous PM, Margaret Thatcher.

Nearing the top, he paused on the plush stair carpet. Thatcher stared imperiously back at him. Her signature helmet of blond hair was preserved for posterity in oils. She had been ousted by her own party. She was too domineering. The public had rioted over her insistence on a poll tax. This gave her enemies the chance they needed. She'd had a long run.

Then his name was loudly called.

"Mister Alex McDonald."

Slight and silver-haired, Sir John Major, the new Prime Minister, regarded Alex through his dark-framed glasses. He was generally regarded as bland, boring and weak. They shook hands. A junior civil servant whispered something in Major's ear about who Alex was. He flashed his false smile and feigned interest.

"How nice to meet you Alex."

They exchanged brief pleasantries. Then Alex was politely passed on to the other guests. They networked furiously over champagne and the canapés. He thought, *Major is totally unimpressive. A junior role in a bank. Then he was Thatcher's yes man. Now he's PM. Interesting rumors about a squalid affair with the dark witch of the party though.*

Impatiently, he returned his attention to Judd.

"And?"

Unflustered, Judd cast his fly.

"We don't need much. Just the occasional chat with our people on the spot in Eastern Europe. They might be helpful to you. We have sources of information that you don't. We need to be sure we're on the right track. You know who's important, who's in and who's out. That sort of thing."

"If that's all, I can agree."

He thought, *Might as well see what they're up to. I'll not tell Becky though. She'd go nuts.*

* * *

Only a few weeks later, Alex was watching CNN in his Prague hotel. The receptionist phoned. Someone was waiting to see him in the bar. He wasn't expecting anyone, but shoved his papers to one side. *You never know. It could be important.*

He stepped from the lift, glancing around. He approached the bar. There was the usual mix of businessmen and high-class hookers. A few of the girls gave him the eye, but he looked away. *Some of these Czech girls are real lookers though. Pity. Still my Becky awaits back home.*

A woman, in a grey suit wearing dark glasses, sat in a corner. She raised them over her head. *My god it's Ramirez. I wondered what happened to her after Buenos Aires. Well, well, well.*

She gave him her warmest smile. Exactly as he remembered, her shining black eyes were inscrutable. He shook her hand. It was warm. She tried to read his face.

"Well Alex, it's been a long time."

"Over ten years."

He weighed up the changes. *Black hair's still silky. There's a cruel hardness to the mouth. Her Mediterranean complexion's kept away most of the wrinkles. One or two around the eyes. A little belly fat, but still looks fit. Still exudes sex appeal.*

He lied, gallantly complimenting his former lover.

"You haven't changed a bit Maria. I often wondered what happened to you."

She pouted accusingly.

"But you didn't even try to find out. Anyway. Let's order some drinks. Then we can catch up."

Warily, he sat down. *She's still hot. Watch out!* When the waiter placed their cocktails, he kept an eye on his Scotch. *I can't have her slipping me something. You never know what she has in mind. She's not here by coincidence.*

Alex insisted on keeping to business. He rejected her proposal that they pool their knowledge in his suite. *It's tempting, but I care too much for Becky for that.*

She hid her angry resentment. *You can't escape Mister. One way or another you're toast.*

They hired a room in the hotel's business center. She shared interesting information on progress in the Czech Government's voucher privatization. Each citizen had purchased books of vouchers at little cost. These were used to bid for shares in the businesses owned by the state. Oligarch owned investment funds were buying up the vouchers from their owners and amassing controlling stakes. Ordinary folk would rather take cash now than wait to see their shares grow in value. They might never do so.

Ramirez showed him MI6 and CIA files on some of the leading Czech players. As always, they had their foibles and indiscretions.

This was useful to Goldring. *There are laws against using insider information. Well, Investment banking's all about getting information before others do. That's just the way of the world.*

* * *

Such low-grade tête à têtes went on for a few weeks. They often met in the British Embassy for security.

At their most recent meeting, Ramirez dropped her bombshell.

"Doubtless, you've heard rumors that there are moves to break Czechoslovakia into two parts."

"Indeed, we have. It is well known that there have always been divisions between the two parts of the country. They date back to medieval times. The Slovaks siding with Germany in World WarII increased these rifts. The Goldring team was so worried we commissioned private opinion polls."

"What did they tell you?"

"They confirmed the anecdotal evidence we had from business leaders. The voters want to keep the country together. 71% of Czechs and 56% of Slovaks."

"Well think again smarty pants. We hear that the Slovak politicians see a whole new country of plum job opportunities. Now they play second fiddle to Czech politicos all the time. With separation they can all get the top jobs. The people are to be persuaded."

Alex was shocked. He hastily scribbled a few notes. This could derail several of Goldring's biggest deals. Besides, they had ignored the Slovak ministers, focusing on where the real power lay.

"Why are the Czechs going along with this?"

"Alex, we know that you've met Václav Havel, the President."

"Yes, I've been introduced at a reception. We also had a business meeting after that. That's confidential."

She tossed her black hair and laughed.

"Would you like me to show you the transcripts of that meeting?"

That caught Alex off balance momentarily. *Wow! MI6 or the CIA must have Havel's meetings bugged.* He nonchalantly waved a hand, to mask his discomfort.

"No need for that. What's your point?"

"He's a symbol of revolution, unity and all that, but a radical playwright as president? That's ridiculous."

"Ha! How did your CIA chums feel when the US chose a B picture actor with senile dementia as President?"

"This is serious Alex. Havel seems hell-bent on encouraging the separation. He's easily influenced on matters he doesn't understand. Unfortunately, that's most things."

Alex pushed back his seat, looking worried. *This is important for Goldring, but also for the people of this region. If the rest of Eastern Europe fragments like Yugoslavia has, there'll be ethnic wars, suffering and mayhem for years.*

"What can be done Maria?"

She moved closer and looked right into his face. Her voice hardened.

"Havel has to go of course. We need to take him out."

His eyes widened in alarm.

"My god! You mean assassination? You must be crazy."

"It's already agreed."

"Why're you telling me this?"

"You're attending a reception with him next week. We want you to slip this in his drink."

She held out a tiny vial of colorless liquid. Thoughts rushed through his head. His palms began to sweat. His collar felt tight. *She really is insane. If I refuse, I know too much. Then what? I'll accept the vial and figure out how to handle it later.*

* * *

Ted Barger, Goldring Silverblatt's Chairman and Chief Executive was in New York. He lounged back in his chair. His highly-polished Oxford's rested on his huge desk. He was on the line to Alex's Prague hotel suite. Alex held the phone away from his ear. Ted had a voice like a foghorn.

"Jesus Christ Alex! If they split Czechland from Slovakia, Goldring could lose a shit-load of money. What the hell's the matter with these idiots? We determine what happens, not two bit playwrights from no-account countries."

Alex winced at his coarseness. *Why do American bosses think crudeness demonstrates dominance?* He gave Ted more details. Ted ended the call with,

"OK I'll have my jet fly me into Prague overnight. Get me an invitation to the meeting with Havel. We'll put the pressure on. We decide these matters. He needs to get that."

* * *

Next day, Ted and Alex handed the security guards their rapidly obtained printed invitations. Goldring's influence had worked again. The invites were gilt edged, embossed and fancy. Ted was angry at guards scrutinizing his passport and having to go through the metal detector.

"Assholes! They need to get a list of important people, so this doesn't happen."

Alex admired the gilded Baroque splendor of the capacious reception hall. *The Czechs are lucky. They were mostly spared allied bombing. The Nazis failed to blow their historic buildings to bits, as they did in Warsaw. Then the Soviets, kept the Czechs short of money. They couldn't afford to bulldoze all this, to erect those horrible Stalinist monstrosities.*

Ted waylaid a surprised waiter.

"Here sonny, gimme some o' that."

Grabbing a canapé in each hand, he guzzled one down. With his free hand, he seized a Scotch from another server. He had shouldered his way past an appalled group to get it.

"OK. Let's go talk with Havel."

The President was polite to Ted, despite his interrupting an existing conversation. As they chatted, Alex looked around to see who was watching him. Whoever was assigned to do that needed to see Alex empty the vial of poison into Havel's drink. *That should delay them from killing me. They surely will, once I do the job.*

He spotted a waiter paying a lot of attention to him from across the room. Then he took a Scotch from another server. Looking furtively about him, he faked sleight of hand. He slipped the poison into it. He moved between Havel and Ted.

"Another drink Mister President?"

As Alex expected, Ted was waving his arms about to emphasize his points. Skillfully, he timed his offering of the drink so that Ted's arm sent it flying. *I hope it looks as though I really tried.*

* * *

After the reception, Ted and Alex headed for the airport in the corporate Mercedes. Alex sat next to the driver. Ted slouched behind Alex in the back. He was venting a tirade at Goldring's head of station.

"I'm not sure Havel understands. He'd better. If you've not had confirmation from his office that he'll block separation by the time I land in New York, I'll get the State Department to fix it."

Alex flipped open his cell-phone to make a call. The driver swerved sharply to miss a cyclist. The phone dropped between Alex's feet. He bent to retrieve it. He heard a crack. A hole appeared in the windshield above his head.

The driver-bodyguard turned hard left, wrenching the steering wheel around. Then he accelerated, burning rubber.

Ducking low, Alex looked into the back between the front seats. Ted's chest was torn open. His head lolled back. His eyes rolled up. Blood pumped everywhere. The big car took another corner in a screech of smoking tires. It heeled over on its soft suspension. The back swung out like a sports car. Alex glimpsed a man falling off his bicycle and pedestrians leaping out of the way. The driver wrestled with the wheel to correct. Alex knew that Ted was dead. He reached for him.

"There's no pulse. He's gone. American Embassy, as fast as you can!"

He glanced warily about him as they raced towards safety. *Was the bullet meant for me or for Ted? There are many who'd like to see Ted gone.*

* * *

In London's Whitehall, the Joint Security Committee was in session. Looking glum, Judd sweated. The Foreign Secretary was in attendance. Judd's boss, the Director of MI6, challenged him. She too was under pressure. Heads were going to roll.

"What the hell's going on? The Yanks are in a tizzy. The hunt for scapegoats is on. They say the President's demanding answers. This is huge. How can this woman Ramirez just disappear?"

Palms sweating, and black eyebrows knitted, Judd desperately tried to cover his lack of information. Eyes bored into him. The Minister gave him an especially hard stare.

"We're searching for her. Whoever did this might have got her. Meantime, our people in Prague have drawn a complete blank on the incident."

His boss snapped at him.

"It's more than an incident Judd. You'd better bloody well find out what's what. We're informed that Alex McDonald was in the car. He's one of your assets. Have you spoken to him yet?"

"He's just landing at RAF Northolt in a CIA JetStar from Prague. They want to have a go at him first. We'll demand to be in on the interrogation."

* * *

The unmarked, small jet streaked towards Northolt. It was the nearest RAF airfield to London. Its narrow fuselage had eight brown leather seats. Two beefy US Marines in uniform were there to ensure Alex behaved himself. He smiled inwardly. *Typical Jar-heads, immaculate uniforms, masses of medal ribbons and service stripes. No necks, shaved heads and two expressions, mean and meaner. I could take them both out in five seconds.*

Alex was already pissing off the CIA Prague head in the opposite seat.

"Listen Pal, thanks for the lift home. It's quite simple. I'm a British citizen. I'm also a senior partner in

Goldring Silverblatt. Our firm has connections in the US Administration at least as good as the CIA's."

The agent shuffled uncomfortably in his seat. The marines put on their extra fierce faces. They looked straight ahead, pretending not to be listening to the arrogant Brit. Their boss tried to bluster.

"We can land at one of several places no one knows. We have interrogation rooms and methods you've never even dreamed about. No one would ever find your body."

Calmly ignoring that, Alex continued.

"Here's the deal. You radio ahead. I want full protection for my girlfriend. MI5 has the details. Roberts from MI5 and Judd of MI6 will be present at our meeting. I'll not say anything till all that's done.

"Oh, and one last thing. I recorded a telephone message before I left. It requires my regular action to avoid it being sent. If anything happens to me, my story will appear in leading media around the world. You need to ensure my safety."

The CIA man looked skeptical. Angrily, he struggled from his seat, dipping his head because of the low cabin. He started forward to make the call from the cockpit muttering.

"I'll pass on your request."

"It's not a request pal. It's a requirement."

CHAPTER EIGHT

A Climate of Fear

"It is vital to find enemy spies who have come to conduct espionage against you. Then, bribe them to serve you. Care for them and instruct them. This is the way to recruit double agents."

Tsun Tzu

"There is nothing more dangerous than security. All spies are untrustworthy. They give a false sense of safety."

Francis Walsingham, Elizabethan spymaster

Alex and his minders rode in the black CIA 4x4 with dark windows. It sped along the A4 road towards London. An identical vehicle was in front and a third completed the convoy. *Hey, they think this is important, or expect me to make a break for it.* There was a beep. The CIA agent took the call. Then, he scowled at Alex, handing him the phone. It was Becky. She was flustered and spoke all in a rush.

"Oh Alex, thank God you're safe. What's happened? Where are you? Three men came to my work. They're plain-clothes policemen. I think they have guns. They drove me home. There's one here now, in my flat. I nearly broke his arm when he accosted me. I think he's mad at me. The others're in a car outside."

"Don't worry. I'll see you later. I'm passing Hammersmith. They want to debrief me. There was a shooting in Prague. I'm perfectly OK. I arranged for the protection. I'll come straight to your place afterwards."

"What do you mean don't worry? You crazy bastard! What've you been up to?"

"Nothing love. Just sit tight till I come round. It's all going to be fine. Look, I've got to go."

He breathed out with relief. Smiling, he rang off. *Trust Becky to deal with the policeman. Bet he got a shock.*

Minutes later, the convoy swung right. It swept through the US Embassy gate, off Grosvenor Square. Several guards rushed forward to open the doors.

* * *

The CIA man hustled the group past several impassive marines standing rigidly to attention. Another agent held open an elevator door. They plunged into the impregnable bowels of the building far below street level. They emerged into a concrete corridor. They walked through an open door into a rather forbidding interrogation room. Alex didn't bat an eyelid. He saw the chair they had waiting for him. Confidently, he walked up to the bright spotlight, shinning into the seat. He reached up and switched it off as he sat down. The men in the room exchanged glances.

Alex noted the presence of Judd and Roberts, as he had requested. He ignored both. Roberts' thick lenses reflected the light.

The CIA's head of station forced himself to make a polite opening.

"Let's talk then Mr. McDonald. As you can imagine, the State Department's going crazy over this. An important US citizen gunned down in a friendly country. Please tell us what happened, in your own words."

Alex decided he'd hold back some of what he knew. *Maybe the CIA was unaware of the plot to assassinate Havel. I can talk to the British intelligence people later.*

"OK here it is. Firstly, MI6 had an agent who exchanged information with me. I suggest you get her back here as fast as possible. She may well know something."

Judd and Roberts exchanged looks of relief and relaxed slightly in their chairs. Alex was going to be discrete. Thank goodness for that. Also, he seemed unaware that Ramirez was missing.

The CIA head asked,

"How do you know that?"

"I don't. She seemed well-informed that's all. Anyway, Goldring must be in turmoil over this. As soon as we're done, I'm going to see Becky. I'll call them in New York on the way there."

Several of those present shifted uneasily in their seats. This guy was a pain in the ass. They needed to keep him till they had everything he knew. The conflicting order was to handle him with kid gloves.

Alex described Goldring's concern over a possible break up of Czechoslovakia. He explained how Ted Barger had come over especially for a meeting with Havel to seek his support in keeping the country together. He could see that all present were already aware of this. No one was making notes, but video cameras were sure to be capturing everything.

"Other than that, you know the rest. We were driving away when a sniper shot Ted dead. Maybe it was the Russians or perhaps some Slovakian separatists. I just don't know."

The CIA head looked incredulous and raised his voice.

"Horse shit! What's on the ta

pe you threatened us with?"

Alex forced himself to relax. His tone was disingenuous.

"Only that I was present when Ted was shot and that I would be interviewed by the CIA. If for any reason, I or Rebecca were not around by tomorrow morning, they should start asking questions."

Judd and Roberts thought there must be more. They remained silent. They could tackle him later, without the CIA.

"If I can think of anything else, I'll call you of course. I'll expect a meeting with you Mr. Judd, about your agent. Please call me to arrange that for the morning. Meantime, you must excuse me. I need to call New York and have to get home to Becky."

He stood up. The CIA head looked pained, but was stuck for anything else to say. He dared not exceed his orders.

* * *

The car dropped Alex off outside Becky's flat. One or two neighbors were twitching their lace curtains, wondering about the comings and goings.

Alex went in. He spoke to the special branch officer inside. The man had a heavily bruised wrist.

"Thank you for looking after her. You should go now."

"But my instructions are…"

"Never mind that. I'll square it with your boss."

He bundled the minder outside. Becky rushed over to him, smothering him in hot kisses. He hugged her tight. Then, putting a finger to his lips, he turned on the radio. He whispered in her ear.

"Don't say anything. They'll have the place bugged."

She looked horrified. He looked through the curtains into the street. In addition to the Special Branch vehicle and two men, he could see a white van close by. He spotted a figure on the roof opposite. *It's likely the CIA is here too.*

He hugged her some more. Speaking very softly into her ear, he told her to wait. He opened the drawer she kept for him. He unzipped a small black nylon bag. Removing an electronic device, he scanned the apartment. She watched him as he identified three bugs. He taped bubble wrap over each. Taking her hand, he led her to the sofa. In a barely audible voice, he told her of Ted's death. She was shocked.

"I need to see British Intelligence tomorrow. Then things'll return to normal. Please just stay here till I get back from that meeting."

She seemed doubtful, but nodded, clinging tightly to him.

* * *

Alex went through the familiar security checks, as he entered the modern MI6 building by the Thames. Judd and Roberts met with him in a secure room.

Judd raised his dark brows and opened the discussion. "Thanks for not discussing your work for Ramirez."

"I don't work for her. We exchange info, that's all. Where is she?

You must have her back by now."

"She's missing. We were hoping you might know."

Alex described his last meeting with Ramirez. Her plot to liquidate Havel, led to a mere flicker of eyes. He tried to discern what that meant. *Did they already know this?* Their faces were impassive. He couldn't tell. He tried a different tack.

"All this is in the tapes for the media. I'm not sure the sniper was after Ted Barger. It could be me they wanted. You'd best keep me and Becky very safe.

"I'll be removing the listening devices from both our flats and personally fitting security devices. Keep the plods on 24-hour watch."

* * *

After Alex left, the others discussed the situation. Polishing his glasses with a silk handkerchief, Roberts speculated.

"Maybe Ramirez was working for the Russians? That's if we believe what he told us?"

"Well, we need to bring her in and find out. Meanwhile, we should tell the Czechs we've found a credible threat against Havel. If the silly buggers allow him to be killed, at least they won't blame us."

Two weeks later Ramirez was still AWOL.

CHAPTER NINE

Reassigned to the Food Industry

"If each person had the right amount of food and exercise, not too much and not too little, we could find the best way to health."

Hippocrates

"Statistics show that of those who acquire the habit of eating, very few survive"

George Bernard Shaw

Alex had chosen to fly on a British Airways, Boeing 747 to New York. He preferred the less claustrophobic flight to a cramped Goldring jet. There were no violent kangaroo jumps like the Concord always made. These were due to tight turns required to meet noise restrictions. *If Boeing had built the thing, these restrictive regulations would never have appeared.* On landing, a corporate helicopter whisked him to the Goldring Tower.

Alex's voice carried great weight at Goldring Silverblatt's Board meetings. He was a huge revenue earner for the company. His reputation was for straight dealing and intelligent action. They always knew where he stood. Still many were suspicious. He was not an American.

Not all the directors possessed Alex's admirable traits. His main antagonist in repeated Board clashes was a man Alex referred to as the Pit-bull in his conversations with Becky. John Bastrani, the Pit-bull, had thousand-dollar haircuts, a pink face and ruthless piggy eyes. They bored into those around him. He was Alex's equal in fee earning. He played golf with the chairmen of most of the S&P's top 100 companies. He had always made it clear that he was after Ted Barger's job and God help anyone who got in his way. The many who had crossed him in the firm had been driven out by Pit-bull's unrelenting and unforgiving campaigns against them.

With Barger gone, Pit-bull saw his chance. He had the backing of half the Board, especially those to whom he had passed fees or helped through some dubious ethical behaviors in the past.

Alex favored another candidate for Chairman. He threw his vote and considerable influence behind his choice. The man was less abrasive, but no less astute than Barger. He was also close to the US President-elect. Goldring's top people always "advised" presidents, whatever party was in power.

As was the Board rule, both Pit-bull's and Alex's candidate left the room, whilst the others discussed their candidacy. Alex voiced powerful arguments. The voting was by secret ballot. His choice won by a narrow margin.

Pit-bull swaggered into the room smirking, expecting to win. When the corporate secretary announced the results he could not hide his fury. Apoplectic, he glared around the room, especially at Alex. When he recovered his mask of composure he congratulated the new Chairman. Meaningfully, he could not help himself but say,

"Well I really hope my friends and clients will continue to give our great firm their full support."

With the new Chairman in place, Alex was asked to address the Board. He beamed warmly around the room. He engaged each person with his personal magnetism. Most directors listened respectfully. Pit-bull fumed, looking down and fiddling with his Board papers.

"Mr. Chairman, colleagues. It seems it would be best for me to avoid further work in Eastern Europe. We have an experienced team in place to continue."

He nodded to a capable woman across the table. She smiled at him.

"Janet here has done a splendid job as head of our global food industry focus. Revenues and profits have grown 25% since she took over. Now, as you all know, she's moving up to an important government role. What could be a better place for her to deploy her industry knowledge and top level contacts than as Director of the Food and Drug Administration."

She enjoyed the approbation and accolades. Alex mused, *The links between the industry and its FDA regulator are too close. That plus the huge lobbying involved are the main reasons why the industry is out of control and in such a mess. She is likely to be a problem instead of part of the solution. Still, she will be an important contact in my new role.*

Alex continued,

"I would like to take Janet's place as head of the food industry focus for the firm."

It was an important job. Most of the major food and beverage industry corporations were Goldring's clients. However, some directors were surprised that he was willing to take this role. He could have chosen a more important one. Vice Chairman or Head of Corporate Finance were examples. Maybe he lacked ambition. They readily concurred with his proposal. It threatened no one. Even Pit-bull looked relieved. He would bide his time. He was determined to get even. He would still become Chairman. This jumped up Brit could not thwart him for long.

Within two days, Alex made an offer on an apartment overlooking Central Park. He hoped Becky could visit. He set up an office in the Goldring Tower. He would keep the one in London and his more modest home there.

Following all this, he commandeered a corporate jet back to London to discuss their joint future with Becky. Speed was more important than comfort. There was no hanging around in queues. With private planes, the crew carried your luggage. Immigration waved you through at the special terminal. He boarded and settled into the spacious seat. They were up and away in ten minutes.

He was worried about how Becky might feel. *She wants me out of this firm. She sees it as the Great Satan of Capitalism. Maybe it is?* He rehearsed his arguments.

* * *

They were enjoying spaghetti carbonara and a second bottle of Barolo in a West End restaurant. Alex appreciated the old-fashioned, straw-bound Chianti bottles, used as candle sticks. Atmospheric murals of sunshine over Tuscany added to the ambience. Becky secretly lusted over the tight little buns of the ever so attentive waiter. *Where do they get those high-waisted trousers?*

She listened dubiously as Alex explained his plans.

"Food is the most important and screwed up industry on the planet. Millions are starving whilst others are killing themselves with over-eating and drinking. The manufacturers are selling them stuff that's bad for them."

He raised a mocking eyebrow and lifted his red wine to her. She laughed. *Maybe she'll share my enthusiasm after all.*

"Nearly half of our clients are involved in food and drink in some way. I include all those in agriculture and production and their myriad suppliers in packaging, processing and advertising. Then, there are the transport and retailing elements. Also, there is this restaurant and catering industry."

He waved a hand around the room. She went over to the attack.

"Fine, but all you'll be doing'll be to make the big companies richer. Goldring always squeezes out the small people, exploits the workers and makes its partners ever wealthier."

Worried, he held up a hand.

"Wait a minute. Give me a chance. Are you so convinced I'm some sort of monster? Let me finish."

She calmed herself and looked lovingly at him. *He's so sexy when he's sharing his ideas with me. Hope he's not planning to take too long. Bed beckons.*

Sensing her relax a little, he resumed his explanation.

"You're right to worry about some of that, but I see the job as eliminating waste, producing healthier food and feeding the world. Goldring will fund a substantial special project from our own corporate resources.

"The Board also agreed to me widening my scope to include elements of all related industries. That means agrochemicals, pharmaceuticals, logistics and much else. I'll need to tread lightly, as other directors lead some of those sectors.

"This special project will be my independent review of how the industry can make healthier and less environmentally damaging products. You would be astonished if you knew how much salt, sugar, nasty chemicals and other muck we eat.

"I've cart blanche to recruit anyone who'll join me for the project."

She saw the light of enthusiasm in his eyes.

"What about us? It sounds like I'll see less of you."

"No you won't I'll be around as much as before and you can also visit the States."

"All right, I can see your mind's made up. Just take me to bed."

* * *

A month later, Alex was still fired up with the excitement and novelty of his new world. Becky and he were sat in her East End rooms. They were sharing their past week's experiences. The lights were down low. Both sipped dry Martinis. The slow beat of John lee Hooker's blues played in the background.

The doorbell rang. He groaned.

"Ignore it love. They'll go away."

Reluctantly, she went to look at the security camera image by the door.

"It's a motorbike messenger. I'll bet the bloody parcel's for you."

She pushed the electric lock button. The door opened with great force. A helmeted and leather clad figure fired two shots from a silenced pistol into Becky's chest. She reeled back, pushing the pistol up with a last supreme effort.

Alex was on his feet, adrenaline pumping. Phut! The assassin let off a round at him and missed. He dodged behind a pillar. The biker moved forward as Becky fell. Alex darted to the right and toward their assailant.

Confused, the assassin shot twice into Alex's reflection in a mirror. It shattered. One bullet ricocheted back into the shooter's face. The figure grunted in pain, turned and fled.

Alex had to make a split-second decision. Give chase, or help Becky? He dropped to his knees by her side. He cradled her head, as her life ebbed away. Her last words would haunt him forever.

"Oh Alex. I love you so much."

He collapsed in a heap next to her body. His eyes filled with tears. Wailing, he hugged her to him, rocking back and forth. All rational thought was gone. He was a heap of grieving emotion and love.

CHAPTER TEN

You Just Have to Keep Going

"Give sorrow words. The grief that does not speak knits up the over wrought heart and bids it break."

William Shakespeare

Alex still clasped Becky tightly to his chest and sobbed uncontrollably. The police arrived in a bedlam of claxons and flashing lights.

A burly constable prized Alex from Becky and hand-cuffed him. He did not resist.

"Come along now sir. We'll sort all this out at the station."

"Becky!"

Alex wailed. The cop supported Alex. He seemed about to collapse.

"Don't worry sir. We'll take care of her now."

They pushed Alex's head down as they bundled him into the back of a patrol car. All the neighbors came out to watch. The woman from the flat next door stood in her curlers looking important. She folded her red mottled arms and puffed herself up. A sympathetic police-woman was taking notes.

"Yes, it was me who called. I saw the front door open and looked in. Bold as brass he wus. She was in a pool of blood. He wus still bendin' over her. I 'ope he gets what's coming to 'im."

A CTV camera was hidden on the opposite rooftop. It picked up all the activity. A Special Branch officer was scanning several screens from a control room in the depths of New Scotland Yard. He alerted his boss. They swung into action. MI5 was informed.

* * *

In the local nick, Alex slumped in the metal interview room chair. His head lolled down. His brain was on fire, twisted in knots.

Two detectives were trying to interview him. The recording tape was on. Others observed from behind the two-way glass wall.

"Come on now, sir. Tell us what happened."

It was hopeless.

Behind the glass, the detective in charge received a call on his cell phone. He reluctantly switched his attention from the interview. He became increasingly frustrated as the call progressed.

"Yes Sir. We've got him in detention. He's been cautioned. We're questioning him now. It seems pretty clear cut. He was still leaning over the body when we got there. There's a witness"

Resignedly, he listened to his orders.

"Oh all right, we'll keep him in a cell till you collect him."

Angrily, he opened the interview room door. The detective sergeant leading the interrogation looked up, annoyed at the interruption.

"Special branch called. They've been watching this bastard. We have to hand him over."

Roughly, they threw Alex into a cell. He was kicked and punched in the stomach. He seemed oblivious to it all.

"You're for the high-jump mate. Best think of thirty years for this."

Uncaring, Alex curled up on the narrow concrete platform of a bed and wept.

Twenty minutes later an unmarked car moved him to an MI6 interrogation center.

A doctor injected him with a powerful sedative.

* * *

Roberts of MI5, Judd of MI6 and a ruddy faced Special Branch Chief Inspector sat in a small conference room. The plain wallpaper and sparse furnishings were typical of MI5. Roberts looked over his thick lenses at the Chief Inspector.

"Right then. Tell us what you know."

The two spooks leant forward with rapt attention.

"We've taken over from the local plods. They got it wrong as usual. The autopsy will confirm, but we think this was a hit by an intruder. The CCTV shows a motorcycle delivery just before the call to the police. The rider ran off in a hurry, holding a hand to his head. We didn't get a look at his face. He was wearing a crash helmet. We're looking for blood in the street.

"We searched the apartment and found Alex's licensed pistol. It's a Glock 27 .40 caliber. It was in a drawer and still in its shoulder holster. All nine rounds were there. It hadn't been fired.

"Our pathologist says the wounds looked small caliber. We found .22 cases. So, it's pretty clear. The autopsy should confirm. We're treating it as a professional hit."

There was a moment's silence as they sat back pondering all this. Judd looked worried.

"Christ! Who did this? Can we assume they were after him? What if he thinks it was us and decides to go public with what he knows? He threatened us before. What if he has stuff already out there in case he doesn't show up in a day or two?"

Roberts looked at both of the others in turn. He spoke in measured tones.

"Yes. Those are the right questions. We should share with him what we know. We need to prove to him that we suspect outsiders. He's made powerful enemies. The French may be involved. Remember he killed one of their agents in Buenos Aires. The Frogs may never forgive him for that."

Thoughtfully, Judd, made a pyramid with his fingers. "That's true and speaking of Argentina, maybe someone in their secret service is after him too. After all, one could argue that his actions led to them losing the

Falklands War. Let's solicit his cooperation in catching them."

Roberts ran with the thought.

"Though that's unlikely, given that the new regime has its hands full, it is possible. We should consider it. One more thing. Have you excluded the possibility that the assailant might have been Ramirez?"

Judd looked dubious.

"She wouldn't have missed. She's been AWOL for a long time now. We think she must be dead."

The Chief Inspector interjected,

"To cross all the Ts and dot the Is we'll put a watch on all the ports for her. We'll have a face scan of her run against all recent UK CCTV records and ask Interpol to look out for her.

"Meantime, we'll see if anyone was after Rebecca Halstead. It was her flat after all. We'll obviously keep the main focus on Alex. This seems to confirm that the attack in Prague was aimed at him and not Ted Barger."

* * *

Two weeks later in a sober suit with a black tie, a devastated Alex stood alone in a pew. His head was hung low. Tears welled up in his eyes.

The small chapel of rest was in Manor Park Crematorium in East London. It stood at the end of a sweeping driveway with peaceful trees and flowerbeds. Monuments and gravestones were arrayed beyond these. The whole place was designed to exude restfulness. In the distance, a broken old woman bent to put flowers on a grave.

Becky's plain oak coffin stood in front of the concealed steel door to the incinerator. As she would have wished, it was devoid of religious symbols.

There were lots of flowers. Alex's tribute was a large heart of white roses. A red silk ribbon inscribed. "I will always love you." was wrapped across its middle.

Becky's mother, her friends and family sat apart from Alex. They blamed him. They knew he was involved in dangerous, secret work. This had to be the consequence.

Unusually, the coroner had taken some of the inquest evidence in-camera. The press was gagged. The bereaved family was furious. They were being kept in the dark. Becky's mother had tears running down her cheeks. She looked daggers at Alex. Embroiled in his own bleak thoughts, he didn't notice.

There was a brief ceremony. Then the coffin rolled behind the opening and on into the furnace beyond.

Alex remained long after everyone else had filed out. Judd and Roberts had stood at the back. They made their discrete exits. As they left, Judd spoke softly,

"Any further news?"

"The Bike was a Husqvarna 500TE, stolen in Bristol the day before. It had false, cloned plates. We've checked all the cameras between there and London and not spotted it. It must have been brought in a van. It's likely dumped in a canal. We are scouring all London CCTV for it.

"Special Branch found blood on the street. The DNA was ruined. A street-cleaner was caught on camera twenty minutes after the biker left. He was squirting bleach from a bottle."

"What did he have to say for himself?"

"It's a dead-end I'm afraid. A person on a motorbike slipped him twenty quid and passed him the bottle. He didn't see the face because of the helmet."

"Shit!"

Inside the empty crematorium, Alex sat remembering Becky, her joy and laughter and their love. Cleaners came and removed the floral tributes. He did not notice.

After twenty minutes, an attendant softly touched Alex's arm. He mentioned that another family was waiting. He gently ushered him out a side door

* * *

As the sleek Goldring jet soared smoothly above the clouds, Alex rolled a sip from his double Glenlivet around his tongue. He enjoyed the smooth warmth of the single malt. He felt the slight tingling of his taste-buds. When he swallowed, the glow passed slowly to warm his stomach. *It always tastes so much better from a lead crystal glass. Maybe private aircraft are superior to big commercial planes after all.*

This one was quite sizable, a new Gulfstream 550. They could be fitted to accommodate eighteen people. Goldring had a fleet of five. Each was fitted to carry only ten in great luxury. Apart from the crew of four, Alex was the only one on board.

He remembered his first corporate jet flight. It was in his early days in consulting. He was bag-carrying for a Kendrick partner. The aircraft belonged to one of their big oil clients. As it taxied past the thousands of other corporate planes on the tarmac at Washington Dulles, Alex asked,

"How come none are emblazoned with their corporate logos? That could build their brands."

The partner smiled,

"Don't you see Alex? None of them want their shareholders or the public to see how well they live"

He wondered what his dad would have thought. *"Well Mister Fancy Pants, dinna let it go to yer hid."*

The day before he decided to return to work, he had heard his dead father's voice, chiding him. *"Son, ye jis have ti get o'er it and get back ti work."* He would never get over Becky. Perhaps work would help take his mind off it.

* * *

In a dusty mud-walled village in Kurdistan, women watched discretely from the curtained cool of their windows. A few goats scavenged around munching on the sparse vegetation. The sun scorched the parched and cracked earth.

Their men-folk were gathering for an important event. A militant leader was to address them.

A cloud of dust alerted them to the imminent arrival of two pick-ups. One ostentatiously mounted a 12.7mm Berezin UB heavy machine-gun in the back. It was pointing skyward. Its turbaned two-man crew scanned the skies for hostile drones or aircraft.

As the small convoy bounced to a halt, the leader scrambled up onto the back of the second dented pick-up truck to make his speech. The men crowded round. Many exuberantly waved assault rifles. One or two brandished RPG 7 rocket launchers

On a distant hilltop, a figure swathed in desert garb hid in the shadow of some rocks. A gently squeezed trigger and the Barret M82 sniper rifle kicked back with a roar. A second .50 caliber round clicked into its breech.

Another shot was unnecessary. The tribal chief no longer had a head. His body was hurled ten yards sideways. Brains and skull fragments spattered the crowd. *I love this gun. How funny they look, buzzing around like angry hornets. They don't even know what happened or where it came from.*

Leisurely dismantling the weapon, the sniper briefly touched a scarred face and strolled to a motorcycle. The machine noisily bounced away along the sheep trails, kicking up stones. *That's another fifty thousand from a grateful Turkish government. Bring on the next contract! If the money's right, I'll work for anyone.*

* * *

Alex arrived back in New York to find the usual bustle. A few offered a little sympathy, but as always everyone was focused on making money There were many huge deals in the offing. Each was worth hundreds of millions in fees to the firm.

The brightest and most ambitious employees were queuing to join his expanded food industry team. Alex was the youngest partner in the firm. His reputation was for involving and teaching his people. Others simply squeezed their juniors dry, riding high on their sweat and creativity. Alex was known to pitch in and do some of the real work.

CHAPTER ELEVEN

The Manifest Evils of the Food Industry

"A leader is most effective when the followers barely know he exists. Once his aims are satisfied, they will say. 'We achieved this.'"

Lao Tzu

In the UK, The Rebecca Halstead case review sessions were decreasing in frequency. In a meeting room, the florid-faced chief inspector watched mesmerized. Judd's beetle brows danced as he spoke.

"So what does Special Branch have?"

Caught off guard, he realized he had not been listening.

"Well, er, nothing new I'm afraid. No new evidence. No sign of Ramirez."

Judd commented,

"Our MI6 operatives haven't found her either. There was a vague and unsubstantiated sighting in Istanbul. It was just before a hit on a Kurdish nationalist. We still think she's dead or gone into permanent hiding."

Roberts grunted.

"Alex has sold his place in London and closed his office here. He's based in Manhattan.

"Sounds like we can downgrade this to a low-level enquiry. We should all keep an eye out in case Ramirez resurfaces. If anything happens to Alex, we should be alerted. Otherwise, we all have lots of other things on our plates. Agreed?"

"Agreed."

* * *

In New York Alex's food industry team got off to a cracking start. For years, the giant corporations had marketed food and drinks, which sold and generated fat profits, as well as even fatter people. Now, they were plagued by the greens, the health nuts and other consumer pressure groups. Law firms were building on their success against the tobacco giants by filing class actions. So far these had failed, fended off by massive corporate legal budgets. Their scientists were bought and paid for. Everyone knew that the dam would soon burst.

Alex recalled Kendrick's specialized food industry teams. Essentially, they tested the products with consumer panels. They kept adjusting the formula, continuing until they found cheaper ingredients that generated taste ratings higher than or close to the more natural original products. Many consumers could not tell the difference between the original and the seamlessly introduced substitutes.

Slogans such as "Healthier" "Less Fat" or "Fewer Calories" added to the appeal of many products. A mixture of higher sales and reduced costs brought in tens of millions for the client. Naturally there were large fees for the consultants.

After participating in one such Kendrick assignment, Alex had kept away from this work. The high levels of salt, sugar, artificial flavorings and colorings involved appalled him. He doubted the veracity of corporate laboratories and external "independent" scientists, who always seemed to find every product safe and healthy. The FDA in the US and its equivalents elsewhere rubber-stamped almost anything.

As his new role expanded into flavor enhancers, insecticides and artificial sweeteners, he became more and more alarmed. *The food industry is just another branch of the chemicals sector.*

As was his wont, Alex started to attend lower level conferences and symposia. This is where he and his team could find out what was really going on. Corporate management and Boards were so many levels up their organizations that they either did not know or did not care what really went on at the coalface.

* * *

That year's World Food Ingredients Conference was held in one of Frankfurt's vast exhibition halls. The list of exhibitors included many of the top corporations in chemicals and pharmaceuticals.

Such events were moved around the world. Each year the organizers would lure industry buyers to attractive cities. They were really there for the junkets.

In Frankfurt, there was the usual tawdry razzmatazz: PR people, free gifts and glamorous demonstrators. There were sleazy private entertainments for important visitors.

This was the perfect place to pick up the gossip from tongues loosened by alcohol. The massive conference center was ringed by many second rate hotels. In a soulless bar in one such, Alex chatted to a salesman from a "coatings" company. He was in an ebullient mood, keen to impress one of Alex's prettier MBAs.

"Let me tell you how it is. Our mission is to sell coatings, right. That means we substitute rusk, breadcrumbs and other cheap stuff for the protein. We lace it with all sorts of other crap to make it taste better.

"This means the manufacturers can use less of the costly fish or meat. The best part is that the coated product is preferred. Kids love 'em. Mums find it easier to get a meal on the table. We get rich. Everyone's a winner."

As he attended such events, Alex noted the behavior of his team members. Those who seemed unhappy with the ethics of the industry and wanted to change things were keepers. Those who saw the industry scams as OK, he scheduled for early transfer.

* * *

Alex liked to debate important issues with his super bright crew. To ensure that the strongest case was made for both sides of any argument, he had separate groups gathering data for or against any specific proposition.

Some of the most important issues, in both the public domain and in the whole industry, were about Genet-

ically Modified agricultural products. Powerful industrial lobbies and enormous advertising and PR expendi-
tures were deployed on both sides of the case. Many in
his team were surprised to learn that large businesses involved in organic food were making claims without scientific evidence and also successfully lobbying governments.

An overarching question was, "Can the world's population of over seven billion be fed without GM agriculture?" Alex's groups debating this issue became quite
heated. He listened to his team members arguing their
points. An earnest young woman was speaking.

"The clear answer is yes. We need to change from
meat and fish to more vegetable protein. We cut con-
sumption in the developed world. Then we end subsidies
to developed countries' farming industries and invest in
underproductive African and Asian farming.

"The latest research shows that in the US where GM
crops dominate, there is an increasing use of harmful
pesticides and insecticides. In Europe where GM is
pretty well banned, crop yields are similar to the US and
the use of harmful chemicals is declining."

Alex noted that one of the brightest of his team, Mads
Peterson, was looking particularly interested and taking copious notes. Alex liked him. From Copenhagen,
blond-haired, blue-eyed and bearded, Mads had a first-
class degree in economics from the London School of

Economics as well as a Chicago MBA. He was a vegetarian and a Buddhist. He rarely lost an argument with others in the team, despite having a soothingly non-confrontational debating approach. He looked thoughtful as the defender of GM reposted.

"Is this due to other factors than the GM crops? Another study shows that if GM was banned worldwide, then the poor countries would see a massive hike in food costs."

In the following team discussion, Mads explained,

"The problem with that is that greedy and unethical GM seed and chemical corporations are destroying the environment with their actions. They ensure that poor farmers have to buy new seeds every season and are sued if they grow their own GM seeds from their original purchase. The most heinous development is the use of herbicides and pesticides that kill everything except proprietary GM crops. The spurious and biased science that their researchers pump out cannot be relied on. No one knows the long-term health effects of residues and contaminated food.

"The poor are already spending 70% of their income on food. They could starve. Some already are. We need to get to the bottom of all this and propose solutions. For example, should GM seed corporations be blocked from owning agro-chemical concerns, due to a clear conflict of interest? We need to find ways to change attitudes and behavior from overconsumption and greed to concern for the environment and the welfare of those in poorer countries."

One of the more pro-business MBAs remarked.

"Oh, is that all we need to do? For all that we would need an unrealistically selfless global society. We all know that the food and agriculture lobbies, striking workers in these industries and the majority of consumers and voters will never support the necessary changes and decreases in their profits and standards of living. The only answer is GM agriculture!"

There were similar rifts on every issue. Some members of Goldring's Board were keen to see where all their research money was going. There were dark rumors about the findings from the project. Alex was called to a special Board meeting. The Chairman warned him of the negative mood. The Board motion in the notice, if passed, would end his project.

He told the Chairman,

"But we aren't ready to report yet. We have no definitive recommendations."

"Be that as it may, you had best offer convincing reasons why this expenditure should continue. There are many who want it stopped."

Alex was worried. He passed the night before the meeting tossing and turning. He saw visions of Becky with bloody wounds, begging him for help. The man whose neck he twisted and snapped in Argentina reached out to him with pleading, hollow eyes. When his alarm wrenched him awake, he was wringing with sweat and more tired than when he went to bed.

* * *

Alex arrived in the familiar Goldring Boardroom for the meeting. As he entered the room, several directors were already in pre-meeting huddles. Some smiled at him, but he noted many would not meet his eye or nervously turned away when they saw him. Several had refused to answer his earlier phone calls. Behind his confident façade, he was seriously worried. Due to his focus on the food industry study, the immediate revenues he brought in had dwindled. Contacts and opportunities were snapped up by others. He had less leverage than before.

The Chairman politely asked him to respond to the motion to kill his project. Alex began, using short film clips and power-point images. He was polished and articulate as always, but felt less assured than he appeared. There was something he detected in the atmosphere, but could not quite grasp.

The first series of film clips showed the polluted seas around fish farms; fields of GM crops utterly devoid of wildlife; a disgusting mat of plastic bottles and packaging covering acres of sea and beaches. The film was chock-full with suffering dolphins, distressed turtles and dying coral. Even the hardest bitten Goldring directors turned away from the hell inside a slaughter house. Alex's commentary included,

"If we don't help our food industry clients meet the demands from legislators to clean up the planet; provide healthy food for the entire world population and find profitable ways forward in the future, there will be no clients or fees for us. We will be living up to our heartless banker image."

As some shuffled uneasily in their seats, Pit-bull sneered, biding his time and never taking his piggy eyes off Alex. The Chairman staved off some persistent interruptions until Alex's pitch ended with,

"We have yet to complete our analysis. I can share this though. We will certainly need to recommend a combination of industry self-policing with intelligently designed regulation. This could include ensuring that those involved in GM crops as well as herbicides and pesticides will have to become separate entities, to avoid the clear conflict of interest..."

Unable to contain himself longer, Pit-bull erupted. He glared at Alex, full of righteous indignation, ire and venom.

"I think we've just about heard enough of this nonsense. If you think our clients want us to get involved in regulation and meddling with their internal ethics you're crazy! No way will those fixing their GM crops to be immune only from their own herbicides accept that. We leave all this nonsense to the hippies, do-gooders and commies."

Several of his cronies nodded. Alex rejoined,

"We'll explain the future scenarios and the clients will see our program as the only way forward. We will achieve something that no single firm or the governments of the world can achieve alone."

"Balls! I've already discussed this with the chairmen of several of my clients on the golf course. They are scandalized that we could even think of such a project. They want this ridiculous effort stopped or they'll dump us, right now!"

Alex and some of the other Board members were shocked. This was a clear breach of Board confidentiality. Someone tried to raise this. The Chairman saw the way the wind was blowing and kept out of it. His survival was on the line too. Effectively, the Board had no choice but to end the project. The vote was overwhelming. Alex stalked out of the room, without looking right or left. Pit-bull was almost dancing in triumph.

* * *

Three weeks later, the lawyers from both sides agreed on Alex's severance package. He was barred from acting for any client as a banker. With the buy-back of his stock and compensation, he walked away with over $300 million.

He hardly cared. The money meant nothing to him. His dream had collapsed. What would he do now?

CHAPTER TWELVE

From the Depths of Despair

"Melancholy and misery are the beginning of doubt...Doubt is the start of despair. Despair is the cruel foundation of varying levels of wickedness."

Isadore-Lucien Ducass, writing as the Comte de Lautréamont

Hour after dank, dark hour, Alex's limbs thrashed around in his New York bed. His whole body twisted in knots. No position granted him sleep. His head throbbed. The hairs on his chest were slicked to his body, silken sheets soaked in sweat.

Half a bottle of malt whisky had failed to either send him into a stupor or erase his phantasms. His mouth was parched, like the putrid bottom of the proverbial parrot's cage. He was too drained of energy to even drag himself into the kitchen to slake his thirst.

Fiendish demons whirled around his brain. He wanted to attack and slaughter them. Somehow, he seemed shackled to the bed, his limbs a dead weight. The loathsome Hatchet-man, who reveled in tossing workers on the scrapheap, his nemesis from his consulting days with Kendrick, snarled at him. The piggy pink face of Pitbull materialized. He had smashed Alex's dream food industry project to save the world. Now, he spewed hatred and manic laughter at Alex.

Worst of all, a version of his despicable self arose before him, the killer in Argentina. The man whose estranged daughters would have nothing to do with him because of his treatment of his ex-wife. Worst of all, he had failed to save Becky, the love of his life, his soul mate. She had given her life for him. He craved bloody revenge, but could not even move. He wanted to blow his brains out for freedom from pain, for peace, for oblivion.

* * *

He spent days in deepest depression; too drunk or too weary to rouse himself. He left separation negotiations from Goldman Silverblatt to his lawyers. They brought the papers to his apartment for signature.

The smart-suited attorneys were surprised and disgusted by the smell of stale booze and body odor in the curtained gloom. Alex's coffee table was covered in dried liquor rings. Empty beer and whisky bottles and filthy glasses littered every surface.

They hardly recognized the red-eyed, haggard, unshaven and barely articulate wreck before them. They failed to see how a man with $300 million to add to his already considerable wealth could be like this.

Not even glancing at the documents, Alex shakily scrawled his signature,

"Can we get you some help?"

"Like what?"

"Maybe a doctor or a friend? Anything at all we can do?"

"No thanks. Just go please."

He clicked the door behind them, not even bothering to use the security locks and collapsed in a chair. He was full of hate, murderous anger and utter misery.

After three days of further heavy drinking and self-torment he remembered something.

* * *

Struggling to regain control, Alex recalled the self-discipline of his martial arts training. It had had a calming effect, enabling him to subdue his anger and aggression. The karate sensei had taught him Zen Buddhist meditations. These dispelled the fear of death and helped manage pain, both in his psyche and in his body. This was an essential part of both Japanese and Korean advanced martial arts training.

Later, he had attended Buddhist meetings in Oxford, whilst he was at university. His wider reading on the subject beckoned from the back of his mind. He remembered that there were other meditations to overcome self-loathing and hatred of others. There was a type of meditation called "Metta," or loving kindness. He decided to look into it further. He showered for the first time in a while and found some clean clothes. He called a maid service to clean the place up.

* * *

Buddhists call a community of monks and lay people a sangha. In New York City, a sangha met in a typical Yoga studio off 52nd Street. It was not too far from

Alex's apartment. It had dimmed lights and a pleasant, polished wooden floor.

He disliked ritual and was skeptical of all religions and spiritual practices. The lighted candles in front of a statue of the Buddha on a makeshift altar concerned him. He hung back, waiting to see whether the devotees were people he could relate too. As they arrived, many said "Hello," and gave him friendly smiles. Some were quite attractive women. That piqued his interest. *Maybe this group will be alright.*

He was pleased to see that there were no bald-headed, robed monks. They always seemed alien to him and certainly out of step with the bustling, mean streets of New York City. A line from Rudyard Kipling sprung to mind. *"East is East and West is West and never the twain shall meet."*

Eventually the teacher entered and took a place by the altar, facing the room. A woman of indeterminate age, she had frizzy graying hair and perhaps some African or Caribbean genes. Her hazel eyes shone with intelligence. A broad mouth lit up with a friendly smile. She settled into the lotus position, matching that of the Buddha statue. Her slight frame was draped in a loose-fitting dress in a brown Asian batik print. Alex felt her personal warmth washing over the room. It was comforting to be in her presence.

She gave a kindly nod to many of the twenty or so people, as they took their places in two concentric semi circles facing the Buddha's statue. The younger ones were cross-legged on raised cushions. Behind them, others, mainly older people, sat on upright chairs. He found a chair at the back, so he could make a discrete exit if this was not for him.

The teacher introduced herself and then looked around the room.

"Perhaps each person who has not been here before can say a few words about themselves and their previous practice. Alex was the third to do so."

"My name's Alex McDonald. I've meditated in the Zen tradition associated with martial arts. Later, I dropped out of a more general sangha in Oxford. I live here in Manhattan and am trying to sort myself out at the moment. Maybe this can help."

The teacher inclined her head in acknowledgement, then moved on to two others. She began the session by explaining that the Buddha taught that all people experienced suffering, illness and death. He developed a behavioral path that could end suffering. None of this was new to Alex.

Next, they meditated for forty minutes. With a short stick, she struck a silvered bell in the form of a deep bowl, resting on a small cushion. As its clear tone reverberated and gradually faded away, everyone relaxed into an upright pose. She invited them to clear their minds of past events and the clutter of thoughts of the future.

To help with this, she instructed them.

"Count your breaths up to ten. Repeat that several times. First count the whole breaths, then the intervals between the out breath and the next in breath.

"Now count the spaces between drawing breath and exhaling.

"Now sense where the breath is entering the body, typically the nostrils. Feel the difference in temperature between the cool in breath and the warmer exhalation."

This process emptied the mind of distracting thoughts. Alex recognized this practice, used in many eastern belief systems, including Hinduism, Yoga and Jainism. As intended, it relaxed him, suspended his anger and inner turmoil, at least for a while, and brought a deep calm. As with his previous attempts at meditation, thoughts, noises and distractions intruded on his senses, especially the wailing of some sirens outside. As instructed, he noted them and they seemed to melt away.

The meditation ended with the teacher striking the bell three times. As its deep resonance drifted into nothingness, Alex stretched. He was relaxed and his mind eased for the first time in days. It was not to last.

The session was followed by cups of tea. He mingled with one or two others and was pleased to learn that amongst them were psychologists, neuroscientists and a student of philosophy. Each seemed to be getting something from attendance over the months, but he could not generalize as to exactly what it was.

After tea, they resumed their places and the teacher read from a Buddhist text. She recounted the story of *The Peacemaker*. Alex shifted uncomfortably in his seat. *Aha, another Buddhist myth. Let's see if there is any merit in the story.*

"The Buddha came upon two armies drawn up for battle over a disputed ridge. He questioned the two war lords as to the agricultural or strategic value of the ridge. There was none. He pointed out that they, the leaders, and many of their valued warriors, may be about to die. He asked whether the men had more value than the ridge. They saw that the combat was not worth fighting and went their separate ways, saving their own lives and those of their men; husbands, fathers and providers."

Alex mused, *Oh if only life were so simple.*

At the end of the meeting, he searched through the box of books on a side table. He extracted a book on Metta Bhavana, the very thing he was interested in. Regarding it doubtfully, he read the cover, *The Karinya Metta Sutra. Why do they use eastern phrases?* The teacher noticed his interest.

"Ah. Loving kindness meditation, my personal favorite."

Alex gave her a twisted ironic smile. "Yep. Do I need this! I feel far from loving or kind. Murderous would better describe my mood."

She looked at his scarred face, sensing his warrior's presence. She could read the lethality in this new member, empathizing with the extreme depths of his pain.

"Don't worry. This can really help you. It helped me. At the next session, we will have a Metta meditation. I hope you can come."

He looked at the ground, unconvinced.

"Thanks, I'll look forward to that."

* * *

Back in his apartment. He reached for the whisky bottle. He stopped himself as he heard his father's voice. *"Y'iv jes got to get over it laddie. Put the bottle down or ye'll kill y'self."*

He replaced the bottle in the bar cupboard and fingered the book. *One thing that really pisses me off about Buddhists is that they keep bleatin' on in ancient Asian languages, Pali and Sanskrit both long dead. Metta Bhavana indeed! Why the hell don't they just stick ta English. That* thought gave vent to a grim chuckle. *Listen to me, the laddie who once resented the English and their "oh so superior" accent. I always wanted to stick to our Scots tongue.* He picked up the volume and started to read.

Ok I get it. This meditation requires silent repetition of certain phrases. Constant recital changes the brain connections, so that the feelings from the phrases become embedded as neural pathways. Then you feel and behave differently.

The meditation begins by wishing good things to yourself. That's easier said than done. I'm the fricking problem, a failure, a murderer, the arrogant man who thought he could change businesses for the better.

Then you think of a close friend. Mmm, do I actually have any o' those? Well there was Hamish back at school, but he turned out to be a bad lot. Still I loved him like a brother. Next, you do the same for an almost stranger. That's most people I guess.

Finally, you focus on an enemy. Plenty of those to choose from. Can this really stop me wanting to slaughter the lot?

He fell asleep easily for the first time he could remember. However, his dreams were of bloody revenge and savage slaughter. He woke sweat-drenched and unrested.

* * *

In her Mandarin Hotel suite overlooking the rice barges and speeding high-prowed boats on Bangkok's bustling Chao Phraya River, Maria Ramirez was pampering herself in the soap bubbles of a Jacuzzi. It had been a difficult, but ultimately successful assignment in Burma's

Golden Triangle. Three dead war lords and CIA money in her offshore bank. She blew smoke rings from her Havana cigar and held a flute of perfectly chilled Bollinger in her other hand. The bottle was within easy reach on the edge of the bath.

She patted herself dry on the fluffy towel before calling down to the spa. A relaxing aromatic massage, from the nice Thai boy they sent up, made her feel great. He offered her "the happy ending" she craved, bringing her to a back-arching and shuddering climax.

Her hotel registration and credit card claimed that she was Juanita Rodriguez. The Costa Rican passport said she was a Mortician. She found that this profession effectively turned away unwanted conversations.

She logged onto her laptop as OzlemZ39*, with a Turkish IP address. It was nice to be connected again after weeks in the jungle. The favorites bar threw up the Wall Street Journal entry from a couple of weeks before. "SENIOR PARTNER AT GOLDRING SILVERBLATT RESIGNS" Her basilisk eyes narrowed and glittered with interest.

She read that Alex had left the firm. Reading between the lines, she concluded he had been forced out. Smirking to herself, she thought. *Is it time for me to pay him a friendly visit? Or perhaps I should let him stew for a bit first?*

A few days later she flew into New York on a Spanish passport, as Isabella Sanchez Ferrez, a pharmaceutical research chemist. She was to attend a medical convention. Her expertly forged green card gained her entry through the shorter citizens line.

CHAPTER THIRTEEN

A Journey and New Challenges

"The whole of the world is the mind's world, the product of the mind."

Chogyam Trungpa - "The Heart of the Buddha"

Alex had a few private meetings with his New York Buddhist teacher. She saw that he needed more time than the twice weekly sessions, and specialist help at that.

"There is a forest monastery in Thailand. I have spoken to the Abbot and explained your need. He's a friend of mine. He has helped many men torn by war. He'd like you to visit them for at least a week. Why not try it?"

Alex was looking haggard, unshaved and wretched after more disturbed nights. He nodded resignedly. What else could he do, except perhaps end it all?

"I'll book my flights."

* * *

He relaxed in a comfortable suite in his favorite Shangri-La Hotel in Singapore. It was a stopover en-route back to New York. His week in the forest had been fascinating. There was an English-speaking monk from New Zealand who helped him. He felt more relaxed.

Still, he had difficulty with the first part of the Metta meditation. How could he ever stop hating himself? He would return to New York with many meditation exercises. Perhaps it was worth persevering.

* * *

In the twisting country lanes around Greenwich Connecticut stood many grand mansions and large estates. Each was hidden away behind walls and high gates, within acres of gardens, paddocks, fountains and the other accoutrements of wealth. Here dwelled those hedge fund managers, bankers and the like, who eschewed the Hamptons and commuted to their offices in nearby Stamford or New York City.

One such house, in traditional colonial style, was especially impressive. Three stories high, it was of white clapboard with a soaring classical portico. A replica of the Trevi Fountain in Rome greeted visitors as they cruised up the sweeping driveway, with its avenue of soaring cypresses. Hidden away were buildings for the staff and for the owner's extensive classic Ferrari collection.

On this morning, the chauffeur of the gleaming black Maybach limousine was sneaking a cigarette out front, waiting for his boss, the Chairman and CEO of Goldring Silverblatt, formerly Alex's ally.

Inside, his boss was dressed ready for work in his $5,000, blue pin-striped suit. He hurriedly kissed his wife and children goodbye and marched through the wide front door, held open by a butler. He moved briskly down the steps to the waiting car. He was expecting to join a couple of his fellow directors at nearby Westchester Airport. They were to fly to Chicago to close a big deal.

* * *

Outside the far wall of the property, a motorcyclist was hidden by some trees from the road. It was a blind spot for the security cameras. The rider pulled off leather gauntlets in order to manipulate the controls of a small drone. Silently, its rotor-blades whirred. It rose vertically, tilted and sped off over the wall and towards the house. Its on-board camera showed the Maybach waiting by the house. The biker deftly maneuvered the drone so that it was partly screened by a decorative pine.

The camera revealed the door opening for the Chairman to approach the car. The rider pulled a cell phone from a pocket in a black jacket. A finger hovered over the send button.

The chauffeur clicked the limo door shut. The watching biker hit send. The car was hurled high into the air. It erupted in an explosion of flames and flying body panels, landing upside down. The thunderous shock wave smashed the drone against the pine. The front door of the house and all the windows were blown inwards. The drone's control screen went blank.

After the wall shook, the biker calmly wiped the prints from the phone, removed the sim card to destroy later and tossed it into a hedge. The rider started the bike. It took off at speed towards the Merritt Parkway.

* * *

Impatiently the Pit-bull tapped his jeweled Pateck Philippe watch, as he sat waiting on the Goldring jet at Westchester Airport.

"He's twenty-five minutes late. Who the hell does he think he is?"

The pilot interrupted the conversation, before his colleague could reply.

"Sirs, I just got a message from your office. You might want to take a look at Bloomberg TV"

Pit-bull pushed the buttons and saw the breaking news on the screen in front of his seat.

"Unconfirmed reports say that the Chairman and CEO of Goldring Silverblatt has been killed by a car bomb, outside his home in Greenwich Connecticut..."

Glued to the screen, the Pit-bull let out a long breath. With a twisted smile, he turned to his fellow director.

"How awful! I guess we'd better head into Manhattan to choose a new Chairman."

* * *

Two days later, the FBI Special-Agent-in-Charge of investigating the explosion was engaged in a tense conversation with London.

Judd of MI6 knitted his beetle black brows. He was flustered by the American's blunt accusations.

"No of course I didn't buy a cell phone in New York or a drone. My credit cards are all here in my wallet. Someone's obviously cloned the card."

"OK, but explain this. Our Bomb Squad has found parts of two explosive devices. They say two limpet mines of British Naval design were attached below the limo. They blew its floor armor apart."

"Look, I've been right here in London all week. Send over the reports and we'll investigate."

"Fucking right Mac! The President's office is screaming for blood."

* * *

Later that day, Judd of MI6 and Roberts of MI5 squirmed in their seats as an apoplectic Foreign Secretary demanded answers. Calming himself, Judd explained,

"We are checking how they cloned my credit card. CRTV at the Walmart store in White Plains, where the items were bought, just shows a figure swathed in a hoodie.

"Both we and the FBI suspected Alex McDonald. He was a Major in the SBS, formerly one of our assets. He had motive. He was fired from Goldring Silverblatt recently…"

The steely eyed Foreign Secretary leaned forward in her chair, interrupting in a menacingly lambent voice.

"Then seize this McDonald bastard and bring him in. The President will be furious if one of your people did this."

Roberts held up a staying hand and looked the Foreign Secretary squarely in the eyes through his thick lenses.

"McDonald could have been involved, though we very much doubt it. He's in Singapore and was in Thailand for the whole of the previous week. Singapore and Thai intelligence services have confirmed that he was in a forest monastery at the time of the assassination. The FBI says he was tight with the deceased. Also he's been drunk most of the time since he was sacked. We hacked into his psychologist's files here in London. He has severe Post Traumatic Stress Disorder from his time in Argentina. Now he hates all kinds of violence."

The Foreign Secretary banged the table and pointedly looked at her private secretary.

"Strike that from the record damn it! You know you can't tell me things like that! So, where the bloody hell does that leave us?"

Judd winced and gave her a reassuring look.

"There are two current lines of enquiry. Maybe McDonald has an enemy who cleverly tried to frame him. The other is strictly entre nous. A close contact in the FBI told me they suspect the New Chairman of Goldring Silverblatt. He hated the previous Chairman and had the most to gain from his death. Obviously, they are handling that with kid gloves. Goldring's share price leapt 10% when he was elected."

Roberts chimed in.

"We are planning to question McDonald very soon to make sure we can rule him out."

* * *

In Singapore, Alex was catching up with the news on his laptop in the Shangri-La Hotel. He was saddened to read of the murder of his former ally at Goldring and incensed to see that Pit-bull was now Chairman.

Then he relaxed. It was all history. His week in the forest had taught him that depression is often caused by people desperately attempting to change the past.

He had more money than he could ever need. What could he do with himself now? There was no point in moping.

The phone rang.

"Mr. McDonald. There is a call for you from London, a Lord Coupar Angus."

Alex had no time for aristocrats. He had never heard of this one. Somehow hundreds of years of peasant ancestry made him reply somewhat deferentially.

"Put him through please."

"Hi Alex, I bet you don't remember me. A voice from the past?"

Puzzled, Alex wracked his memory for the familiar slightly accented English.

"It's Jaimie Ferguson from the karate dojo and Glasgow Royal Marine Reserve."

"Hell Jaimie, course I remember. What's this Lord Coupar Angus nonsense?"

"Ha. That's me. I built up a property empire and donated tons to the Tory Party. In return, I was made a life peer. I sit on the Joint Parliamentary Defence Committee. That's how I managed to track you down. You were a hard man to find.

"Listen, I also chair an executive search firm in London. We have a job right up your street. You can finally set the world to rights."

It would be nice to see Jaimie again. Besides I need to do something with myself.

"OK I'll fly over."

"That's grand. How about lunch in the House of Lords Friday? What's your email? I'll confirm the details."

* * *

On the long flight to London, Alex tried to relax, but thoughts of Becky and his anger at those he felt had damaged his life intruded. Ultimately, he blamed himself for his own misfortunes. *I'm a nasty piece of work to be sure. Maybe I can find something to do to make amends?*

He approached passport control at London's Heathrow Airport in a subdued mood. The turbaned and bearded Sikh immigration officer scrutinized his face and then his computer screen. He beckoned to two men lurking in the background.

"Excuse me Mr. McDonald. Please just step this way for a moment."

Oh shit. What on earth now?

The muscular Special branch men took him by the arms and firmly led him through immigration. They told him his luggage would be sent on. He was bundled into a black car, which set off at speed.

CHAPTER FOURTEEN

Can I Create Order from Chaos?

"Don't hire a man who does work for money, but he who does the job for the love of it."

Henry David Thoreau

After a sticky interview with MI5 and a stony-faced FBI observer, Alex felt he had convinced them he was not involved in the Connecticut murders. They raised their eyebrows, when he proposed that the chauffer's life was of equal importance to that of the big banker. That man had family too. These were not the values they lived by. They served the rich and powerful leaders of the state.

They seemed fixated on the idea that the perpetrator had some connection with him. He was unable to help them as to what it could be.

Misguidedly, they kept the information about the assassins escape on a motorcycle to themselves, so he was oblivious to the possible connection with Becky's death.

* * *

Two days later he was passing through the elaborate security into the Palace of Westminster. He was on the way to meet Jaimie, Lord Coupar Angus, for lunch. Despite previous visits for receptions, meetings with committees and luncheons with ministers, he was always impressed by the whole Ruritanian charade that was the British system of government.

Any foreigner would instantly recognize the mainly 19th century Big Ben and Parliament buildings overlooking the River Thames. Insiders passed the statues of great men and the arts and crafts style floor tiles and decorations of the octagonal central lobby.

Jaimie appeared from the direction of the Lord's Chamber and greeted him with a warm handshake. Alex recognized the same small man who defeated him in the Glasgow Karate dojo many years before. Time had been kind to Jaimie. There was graying hair, but apart from a slight paunch he looked fit and healthy.

As they entered the House of Lords' dining room, Alex was once again bemused by the gaudy yellow and rather gauche wall coverings. Lords did not necessarily have good taste. The dark wood-paneled ceiling, red leather chairs and white clothed tables were as he remembered. On other occasions, he had met ennobled ministers and business leaders there. He recalled that the food was mediocre. *Still, I'm not here for that.*

They threaded their way toward their table. He noted the usual mix of lords and guests. He spotted former ministers and prime ministers booted upstairs from the Commons. There were businessmen who, like Jaimie, had donated to their chosen parties in return for the prestige, connections and influence. *In the 21st Century, why are many still impressed by royalty and titles? Maybe it's because the rich buy or inherit them?*

When feeling extremely bored, he sometimes watched the BBC Parliament Channel. The usually sleepy Lords' sittings were one big yawn. *One aged person droning on to those who remembered to attend. Some slept in their red leather benches. Others chatted amongst themselves, or wan-dered in and out as if in the fog of advanced dementia. It's rather like being in a geriatric home, where all the patients feel they are somehow relevant. Annoyingly, these unelected timeservers play a role in lawmaking.*

He remembered a quotation from Karl Georg Büch-ner, "The breath of an aristocrat is the death rattle of freedom." As they sat down, he turned to his friend Jaimie and gave him a wholly insincere grin.

"Well thanks for the invite, I hope your conversation is a whole lot better than the debates. Oh, and I've never actually seen you in the house."

"Och come on! My attendance record's better than most. Anyway, this is the most exclusive club in Lon-don."

They ordered. Jaimie toasted Alex.

"To the unsung hero! I heard something of your ex-ploits in Argentina."

Alex looked around to see if anyone was listening.

"Well few have, thank goodness. I wish I could have told my dad before he died. He never asked. Whatever, I'm not proud of most of it. Its best left buried. I still have nightmares."

"OK. Well then, how's your sex life."

"Terrible. Why? Are you offering me your body Jaimie?"

"Ha! I'm happily married pal."

"Congratulations! Is he a sailor or a marine?"

They exchanged further banter and happy memories. As they waited for desert, Jaimie finally raised the opportunity he brought to the table.

"As I mentioned, I'm the Chairman of the London unit of a global executive search company, KZW. We have 115 offices around the world."

"Aha, headhunting."

"Exactly, but they try to avoid that term. The firm's been in decline since the 1970s. They neglected their brand, technology investments and fired the last two CEOs after just a few months each. They also nearly went bankrupt, due to over expansion and high overheads. They squabble all the time. Globally it's a mess, but it works well in many countries."

"Mess is good, but why would I be interested? You don't want me to buy it do you?"

"Let me ask you a question. What is the highest level of strategy?"

"It's a tricky one, but I'll share my view. It's Corporate Finance. Business leaders can do their best, but behind the scenes are always money men. They lie in wait to take the business over, break it up and force it to perform better. Been there. Done that."

"Let me challenge your proposition. The team at the top is the key to everything. That's true of any enterprise."

"Hang on. That's nonsense. Too many leaders forget that no one succeeds without taking their employees with them."

"OK, I'll grant you. the key to performance goes all the way down to the clerk in a cubicle or to the maintenance man with a screwdriver. But the whole team needs building top-down. Getting the right top team is the first step and the highest level of strategy. That team develops plans and is responsible for their execution throughout the organization. That's what we do. We find the top team. It's also great fun. We work with the most important businesses all over the world, for governments too. No one refuses a call if they think they are being tapped for something more important."

"OK, you've got me intrigued. I suspect you've used this pitch before a few times, haven't you? But why me?"

"Now, I wouldn't want you to get big-headed, but you take on almost impossible challenges and usually succeed. You have experience, affinities and contacts in all the major world economies. You can square root any business very quickly. I expect you are a good judge of people."

"Well that's all very kind of you, but I've often been wrong on the last point. You're right about difficult challenges, but they do have to be at least possible. Is this one?"

* * *

Alex decided to meet as many of the office heads of KZW Worldwide Search Inc., as possible. I'll see if being in their CEO role is of interest. The surname initials of the three, long-deceased founding partners formed the logo and name of the enterprise.

He took two months for a round-the-world trip. As he traveled, he mentally noted the problems.

He visited the thirty largest KZW offices and the headquarters in Chicago. This HQ team is beyond redemption. The offices are a pigsty, with dirty windows and half-eaten sandwiches lying on desks, covered in chaotic heaps of papers. They are a miserable and disillusioned lot. Rudderless and badly led, they never complete projects.

A key candidate database system had been in development for several years. There was no end in sight. Marketing was underfunded and badly managed. He was especially unimpressed by the Marketing head, John. He's a pleasant person, but hopelessly unqualified for the job he's failing to do. KZW's brand recognition and positive perceptions have declined over many years. I'll keep this to myself for now, but he'll have to go.

In the international offices, the leaders were as keen to meet him as he was them. They did not trust their own directors to make the right choice, because their last two picks were a disaster. They made this very plain to Alex. A partner in Singapore summed it up.

"We are a search business for Christ's sake. Yet we cannot even choose good people for ourselves."

Alex's experience at Goldring Silverblatt had taught him that working owners were always ready to be critical and vociferous about anything they did not agree with. During his odyssey, they spilled out their concerns and dissatisfactions. This made his diagnostic task much easier.

On his travels, Alex was impressed. They certainly have the connections and client lists. They seem pretty wealthy too. The New York senior partner had a painting of his 80-foot yacht on his wall, striped spinnaker straining in the wind. One of the Madrid partners collected Bugattis. The Brussels office showcased original paintings by Picasso, Tanguy and Miro on its walls.

Each partner and office head has a distinctive and powerful presence. Most are smooth operators who show a great interest in the person across from them. Some, like the Sidney and Melbourne partners, were bluff, no nonsense tough guys, with pretty basic humor and very into sport. They reflect the culture of typical Australian mining and banking clients. I've met the type

Each visit added more pieces to the jigsaw. The picture explained why such a prestigious and once dominant firm was rapidly fading against its competition. There were long lists of complaints, about the incompetence of their own Board. *This company has allowed every office to do its own thing, to fragment. There's no unity of purpose.*

The partners harked back to better times. Many of the business units feuded with each other over leads, accounts, territory and split fees.

* * *

Alex walked through the doors of the Paris office, high in the ultra-modern Tour Granite in La Defense, the business district.

A chic receptionist gave him a bright smile and welcomed him in heavily accented English.

"Ah Yes, Monsieur McDonald. Welcome to KZW Pari. Ze Contessa-Brecht is expecting you."

Several of the KZW partners had alluded to the Contessa. Remarks included,

"Be careful what you say to her. She's very powerful and not to be crossed."

"You have a treat in store."

"Count your fingers after the handshake. If there are more than two, she likes you. Then you're really in trouble."

He was also intrigued by what he had read about Alice Contessa-Brecht. Though he had no truck with aristocratic pretensions, he recognized that many clients did. His research revealed that she was French born. Her father had been Minister for Agriculture. Her mother was Italian and her step-mother a German aristocrat. She had graduated from the elite ENSMSE, École Supérieure des Mines de Saint-Étienne. Established in 1816, this was a leading university for business education.

She appeared to have several Italian and French noble titles, but used that of her Flemish first husband, a Belgian aristocrat. He had died in a yachting accident a year after their marriage and six months before her second. That's interesting. I wonder…? Come on Alex, be nice.

Now, she was married to the CEO of a leading Aerospace Corporation. In classic French style, he had previously been a junior minister in the Defense Ministry. Such switching between government and industry together with state stockholdings ensures the ability of the Fourth Republic to continue the mercantilist control of all key businesses that's lasted since Colbert, Louis XIV's Finance Minister.

The KZW website claimed that The Contessa focused solely on finding Board members for international companies. He suspected that of the many in search firms who claimed that, few really did. I wonder if it is true in her case. On paper, she seems the sort that would.

Before she stepped from her office to greet him, he was struck by a hint of a pleasant and aromatic smell. It somehow unsettled him. What could it be? Jasmine?

As he shook her hand, it became clear. It was the Contessa' subtle scent. Not Jasmine, maybe oleander and ylang ylang flowers? There was something else that aroused feelings of both sex and fear. Maybe that's just her pheromones?

Her handshake was strong, though unsettling, as if she was probing for a weakness in his wrist, testing his body. She gave a hint of a smile. He noticed a large blue baguette-cut diamond ring and well-muscled arms. She had been on the French Olympic swimming squad some years earlier. I can believe she's a sixth dan aikidoka. That was listed under her other interests. Wow, glad she chose not to break my wrist. She certainly could.

The olfactory titillation and latent power of her grip proved just an overture to her visual crescendo. She was a shapely blonde, with emerald eyes that seemed to transfix him. They drew him into their depths, like whirlpools. Her business suit was perfectly tailored to her shapely body. Her jewelry was understated, but clearly expensive. Her face was unlined and belied her 52 years. He would have guessed 35 maximum. She must spend a fortune on her appearance, likely including cosmetic surgery. Odd she didn't change the aquiline nose;

though its distinctive hook gives her an even more aristocratic hauteur.

She gestured to an easy chair and a low table set with a Sèvres coffee set for two. It glistened with gold. She sat down genteelly, revealing shapely calves. I can't quite place the accent, slightly Italian perhaps and a little breathy. It reverts to a French one when she's excited.

"Oh Alex, I'm so pleased you could come. Let's have a coffee. Later we'll have lunch. I have cleared the day for you."

He was impressed by her knowledge about him. That seemed common to all the partners he had met. It shows they did an excellent job of research, as one would expect in their trade. There was something he could not quite trace behind her latent sexuality and warmth towards him. He was slightly unnerved by the light touches of his arm. Is she coming on to me or is there something sinister behind the smiles and verbal stroking? She's intelligent, witty and amusing, but I feel threatened. Wow!

Alex found that asking people about the successes of their business was a great way to get them to open up. It worked now, at least a little.

"Have you had many recent successes in recruiting CEO's for large organizations?"

She puffed herself up and spoke enthusiastically, emphasizing her points with Gallic shrugs, lip pursings and emphatic hand gestures.

"But of course, mon ami, that is my main activity, as well as being on the global Board of KZW and running our French and Belgian operations. Others focus on senior executives. I 'ave placed three directors at Électricité de France this year, including the chef of a large division. Last week I placed a Directeur Général for BNP Paribas. I think I close about twenty such appointments every year. It is because I 'ave ze top contacts in the government and French and Belgian industry."

"That's great. So how does that compare with other BKW offices?"

"Ouffe, we are ze best of course, but zere are a few strong offices, New York and Shanghai for example. But KZW 'as many problems. In some places our local partners 'ave not done much. Ze US is a big disappointment. They spend more time fighting each other over oo does what than winning business. They operate at too low a level. Our 'edquarters is in Chicago. This iz ridiculous. Most people there cannot even see the coasts of the US. Zey speak only American and know little of ze rest of the world."

"What do you think needs to change then?"

"Well we should start by closing many offices and opening better ones, especially in Asia. We should only 'ave top people. 'Alf ze Board of Directors would be gone if we did zat."

She continued to share her ideas, damningly criticizing most of the Board and several other prominent partners, especially the Chairman. It was a particularly useful interview. Lunch at the Michelin starred La Table du Lancaster could only be described as one of the most exquisite meals he had ever had. I feel I've made a hit with her, but that there was a slyness and reserve behind the way she smiled. She seems by far the best KZW partner I've met so far.

* * *

Later that night in her palatial Paris apartment, the Contessa luxuriated in the caress of the silk sheets on her toned thighs. Sighing with satisfaction, she looked up to the exquisitely pleated canopy of rich fabric above her head.

The sheets were scented with rose petals, according to her strict instructions. It was pleasant after the stench of sex, sweat and pain left in the secret room behind the red leather-covered door at the far side of her bedroom.

She reviewed her day. It had been somewhat mixed. As expected, Alex is a clever and intriguing man. As we shook hands, I felt a worthy and surprisingly strong opponent. Normally my type is 30 years younger and subservient, but somehow, I want to 'ave him. The scars on his face must be from what my friends in our Foreign

Office in Quai d'Orsay told me about Argentina. Apparently, he is a killer. 'Ow exciting. It would be fun to control him like a stallion and rake blood across is back with my nails.

As friends at Goldring and Kendrick Paris shared, Alex is indeed a powerful businessman, but with the fatal flaw of naïveté. Their consistent story is that he is anti-corruption, always tries to find the best in people and believes that businesses should be totally ethical. The question that remains is, should I block 'im from getting ze job or can I manipulate and use him to win what I want? Maybe I should relieve him of some of the fortune he 'as. I will consider zese things, but I am tempted. E 'as a cute meaty derriere.

Her evening had not gone so well. Fired by lust for Alex, she had been ready for a good session with her current chauffer, behind the red door that led from her bedroom to a sound-proofed chamber. What a disappointment. She had handcuffed the initially willing victim to the bench. Her whip had drawn blood, but when she flipped him, he just sniveled and shriveled. He would have to disappear like so many of the others. Quel dommage. Anyway, she was grooming her tennis coach to be next in line.

* * *

Alex was pleased with his trip to Paris and flew on to Germany. The German KZW main office was in Düsseldorf, but because Germany had no dominant business center, like France or London, he would be visiting the specialist hi-tech office in Munich, the government focused team in Berlin and the manufacturing specialists in Stuttgart.

He looked forward to savoring the delights that each city had offered in the past. This included renewing his acquaintance with the dark Düsseldorf Altbier and the crispy Sweinhaxe of Munich. I can almost sniff the smell of succulent pork and crunch the crispiness of the crackling. The only way to eat the pig's foreleg is to pick it up and gnaw at it, a delightfully messy experience.

His friend Jaimie had advised him to arrive in the German head office early in the morning.

"The Geschäftsführer and Deputy Chairman of our global business in Düsseldorf is rarely sober after lunch. You'll like him; he's a jolly and knowledgeable fellow."

As he settled into his airport hotel bed, Alex felt pretty good about his encounter with The Contessa. I'll need to control myself to keep this on a purely professional basis. In his dreams they had wild sex.

CHAPTER FIFTEEN

Jack be Nimble—Jack be Quick

"It's curious that physical courage should be so common in the world and moral courage so rare."

Mark Twain

Alex waited in KZW's ultra-modern lobby in Chicago's prestigious, hundred-floor John Hancock building. This was KZW's headquarters. The non-executive Chairman, Jack Clarke was also the head of the firm's Chicago operations.

As Alex waited to be shown in to meet Jack for his interview, he focused his mind on what he had learned of the man. Online research had yielded some bare bones. Jack is 75 years old. He was a graduate in accounting from a mid-ranking state university. He joined a small accounting firm in Chicago and was an audit partner with them. They sold out to a top-four global firm. As part of the deal, Jack became one of thousands of their audit partners. Otherwise his education would have denied him entry.

He stayed there for twenty years and then left rather abruptly. The reasons are not available. He has been with KZW for twenty years and was elected to the Board ten years ago. He became Chairman five years after that. He claims expertise in Board searches and Corporate Governance. He sits on two small firms. In one he is the Chairman.

To Alex's surprise Jack had almost no public profile in the media. As Chairman, one could have expected TV appearances, speeches at major conferences and articles in the business press. I see his Curriculum Vitae, but he is somewhat of a black hole beyond that. My interview with Jack, plus the opinions of others I have interviewed, must serve to complete the picture.

Alex had met all the Board members on his travels. He compared each interview to his own observations. There are three big beasts in the KZW menagerie. Each attracts both opprobrium and supporters.

His meetings with KZW's key players confirmed that they did not like each other very much. In some cases it was full-blooded hatred. As he had found in other partnerships, the more powerful people were in the politics of the firm, the more critics they had from those clawing their way up.

Other partners around the world had expressed polarized views about Chairman Jack Clarke. Alice, the Contessa, clearly loathed him. She saw Jack as a rival in the power struggle to influence and control the Board. Other Europeans had expressed mixed views. Alice's enemies sided with Jack.

The Asia Pacific partners don't like Jack at all. Their main complaint is that he runs the firm for the benefit of the American offices. Despite this, the US business had failed to grow and trailed all their major competitors by every measure.

Unwisely, Jack had made remarks as to the instability of the rapidly growing Asian markets. The Asian directors claimed he never visited their countries. He had no understanding of the world outside the US.

The US partners gave guarded responses. They seemed to fear that their views might get back to Jack. They were only mutedly supportive. All of them voiced a dread that there could be a non-US Chairman if Jack retired. They saw him as the man to keep real power away from the Europeans. Europe generated 60% of the business, against only 17% from the US. Alex wondered. Perhaps that is because they have a 75-year-old, lack-luster Chairman, who has let everything drift for years.

Alex recalled meeting the KZW director from San Francisco. The man resembled a caricature of the typical US Senator. His swept back, silver grey hair was meticulously and expensively groomed. The fixed white smile was due to his American jaw resplendent with implants. A finely chiseled cleft chin jutted with determination. He spoke especially well of Jack and he particularly praised the performance of Marketing in the Headquarters operation. Alex had written in his notes. "Why? Our analysis shows KZW's marketing as exceedingly weak." This was a question that he would need answering before long.

He had added some notes to the bare bones after the other meetings. Jack had been married three times. His current wife of ten years had been an audit clerk in the accounting firm and had joined him at KZW. A rather hefty woman from her photograph, she was now a full partner and number-two in Chicago. Perhaps their relationship had something to do with them leaving the audit firm? He had two adult sons from an earlier marriage.

The secretary came to shepherd him to the interview. As he walked to the room, Alex tried to clear all this from his mind. *I mustn't prejudge the man.* It was 4:30 pm.

* * *

Alex was ushered into Jack's large office with a view over Lake Michigan. Far below, the sun glinted on the wings of a small plane taking off from Midway airport. He could tell a lot from a person's office. Jack's was meticulously tidy, with no documents around. There were gifts he had received from various KZW offices. There was a wall of group photographs with Jack at the front and center. They seemed to be from KZW conferences. *Does he have a life outside KZW?*

Jack was courteous and friendly. *His thinning hair is suspiciously jet black.* He was tall, gaunt and thin, looking. At least ten years older than the pictures in the firm's brochure. Chuckling, he immediately offered Alex a drink.

"Well, the sun must be well under the yard arm somewhere in our empire. I'm going to have a Scotch."

Surprised, Alex smiled. *I wonder if he's a lush. A couple of directors hinted at that.*

"Er thanks, I'll have the same."

His host poured two stiff Glenlivets into cut-crystal glasses. Alex winced as Jack destroyed the flavor with ice. *I do wish Americans wouldn't do that and at least ask me how I wanted mine.* Jack set the bottle down on the small table between their easy chairs.

The discussion struck Alex as very professional, apart from the several refills of Glenlivet during the meeting. As with the other KZW people, Jack had done his homework in checking up on his career. When Alex answered questions about his contacts and experiences, Jack boasted about his own clients and experiences. *A sure sign of insecurity.*

Jack was keen to show off his expertise in Corporate Governance. His explanations were like paragraphs from a textbook. *It's clear he's a stickler for form over substance. There's an odd underlying nervousness.*

He was clearly worried by Jack and rather defensive in all his responses to his questions. *In essence, he's saying that all is well under his leadership and maybe I'm too qualified for the job.*

* * *

The next day, Alex returned to the John Hancock to meet other partners in Jack's office. The boss did not arrive till

10:00 am. He stuck his head around another partner's door looking both suspicious and hung over.

"Is Mary looking after you? Do you want me to sit in?"

"No don't worry. Everyone is being most kind. I'm sure you have all the important matters to deal with from running a worldwide business."

When he had gone and the door was closed, Mary confided,

"Nothing happens here without Jack's knowledge."

Like Jack's other colleagues, she was otherwise tight-lipped, despite Alex's probing. Many times he was stonewalled with,

"You'll need to ask Jack about that."

He obviously rules with a rod of iron. In which case, he's responsible for the mess this company is in. No wonder he doesn't want me around.

CHAPTER SIXTEEN

The Tiger's Lair
"In what distant deeps or skies
Burnt the fire of thine eyes?"
William Blake - The Tyger

Alex's final interview before he returned to Chicago to meet the full Board was in Hong Kong. He always liked the bustle and buzz of the City. The gateway to China and now part of it, but so different from the rest of it.

He was especially looking forward to meeting Robert Lee-Soames, KZW's Board member, who headed a spectacularly successful office there. Alex's research and other KZW meetings had whetted his appetite for this meeting.

Lee-Soames English father had been a director at Jardine's, one of the famously huge conglomerates, or Hongs. These were built during the days of the British Empire, based on the opium trade and powerful connections. Robert's mother was Chinese. He was born in the then Colony. The family had made a successful transition to Chinese rule.

Lee-Soames had boarded at Harrow School in the UK. It boasted many

distinguished alumni, including Winston Churchill and Benedict Cumberbatch. Lee-Soames was the Captain of the school rugby team there. He went on to gain a master's degree in computer science from Heidelberg University and an MBA from Stanford. He also claimed to speak six languages. A keen golfer, he was a director of the prestigious Hong Kong Jockey Club.

Prior to KZW he had started a successful high-tech business. When he cashed out six years later, he launched what had become KZW's Hong Kong office.

Other partners spoke about Lee-Soames with awe. Some thought he wanted to take ownership of the whole firm. Others envied his success, as their own operations teetered towards decline. A partner from Shanghai, an American, had spent an afternoon with Alex drinking Moutai. The fiery spirit loosened the partner's tongue. He called Lee-Soames the smiling Tiger, waiting to gobble up KZW.

"Charming guy. I wouldn't trust him an inch. Bob sure has the connections though. Some of his people are senior Communist Party Members, with tentacles in Beijing. He knows everyone of importance. There are even rumors that this includes the heads of the Triads, our gangster families. I wouldn't want to cross him, that's for sure. You won't tell him I said any of this will you."

Alex knew that colorful, larger than life characters were big winners in advisory services. Clients preferred those who were interesting, amusing or even eccentric. They liked to socialize and play golf with such personalities in investment banking, consultancies and headhunting firms. The money spent on lavish entertainment is from their corporations or paid for through the advisory firm. The firms make up the costs through their charges.

This form of corruption is widespread and largely invisible. Been there. Seen that. Done it myself to my shame.

* * *

Alex was admiring the superb collection of Chinese porcelain in KZW's Hong Kong lobby. He was captivated by an exquisite pair of Tang Horses. They're the largest I've ever seen, resplendent with green and brown streaks in their glaze. The horses stared back at him from behind their security glass. A deep but smooth voice, with an English accent resonated behind him.

"Do you like them? My father gave them to me for my 21st."

Lee-Soames held out a large meaty hand, as Alex turned a little startled.

"I'm Robert, you can call me Bob. Do come through."

Bob had an amazing presence. He was a big man and heavily built. A burgeoning paunch implied that his rugger days were long over. His eyes seemed to be nearly twice normal size and were a strange amber in color. He appeared to be watching his visitor as a cat observes a mouse. His skin had a Chinese tint and he had typically Asian black hair. But the round face and long nose are not easy to place. Dark bags under his eyes hint at a dissipated lifestyle.

He must have suffered bullying at school. Other boys would have picked on him as a foreigner with strange appearance. On reflection though, Maybe Bob became the bully. He must be intimidating to some. If real, those Triad connections would be scary.

The meeting room was entirely decorated with Chinese antiquities, including intricately carved Ming Chairs and a large table. A golden statue of a roaring tiger dominated the room from a sideboard. Its fangs were bared in a snarl. As Alex glanced at it, Bob smiled, showing his own teeth.

"Ah, I was born in the year of the Tiger. It is considered lucky for a man. For girls, it's bad luck. They find it difficult to marry. They might devour their husbands."

A stunningly beautiful Chinese woman, in a figure hugging cheongsam, poured tea from an ancient teapot. Its incredible patina marked it as another valuable antique. The silk fabric of her dress was slit to the thigh. As she served him. I wonder if the rumors are true as to Bob's many mistresses. He is said to entertain them three at a time on an ocean going Junk while cruising round the islands in the Pearl River Estuary. There was a painting of the heavily gilded vessel on one wall. It must be 90-feet long.

Alex felt the meeting went well. He liked Bob, but remained concerned about some of what he saw and heard. On the positive side, Bob was from Alex's world. He is highly intelligent, with charisma. He spoke easily about the big corporate moves open to KZW.

"We could clean it up and go public as our competitors Korn Ferry and Heidrick & Struggles did. Or, we could raise the capital and reverse into one of those two, when we've bought one of them. I hear you have the funds to do that yourself, if you feel so inclined."

Alex thought Bob was teasing him and smiled.

"Why haven't you done that?"

Alex saw that Bob was trying to win him over to his views. Bob explained why he joined KZW.

"We needed a global network to bring US and European clients to Hong Kong and China. Few Chinese-owned companies use headhunters. They prefer the tightness of family members. Things are changing though, especially when they want to take over Western companies based in the US or Europe. In retrospect, I feel I made a bad choice in merging with KZW two years ago. KZW looked good from the outside, but it's a shambles once you cut through the PR and bullshit.

"If they cannot sort themselves out, I will pack up and leave."

"But you are on the Board and therefore have some control."

Bob just smiled enigmatically.

"You'll see."

They spoke for several hours, including dinner at the Yacht club. Alex liked Bob, but wondered about his motives and plan for the end game. Bob had left a threat on the table. If he were to leave KZW it would leave big gap in revenues and the office network. Obviously, he wanted Alex to make the reforms he deemed necessary.

CHAPTER SEVENTEEN

Picking a Winner

"No one said this was going to be a fair fight. Business fights never are."

Alton Blomquist

"I know he is a good General, but is he a lucky General?"

Napoleon Bonaparte

A few days later, Alex's limo driver pulled in at the forecourt of the Drake Hotel in

Chicago. The chauffer swung his door open. Porters clustered around the open trunk to extract his luggage.

It was a typical Chicago January and 20 degrees below. The external heaters blew down from the ceiling of the entrance canopy. They warmed guests as they stepped in from the icy cold. Nonetheless, the Drake's outside crew were bundled up. Their uniforms included gloves, heavy coats and fur hats, as they exhaled steam into the frigid air. He was glad to move swiftly through the main doors and into the elegant lobby.

Alex always stayed at the Drake. I like hotels with character and a plush traditional style. Besides they know me here. Most modern American hotels are the same all over the world. The bellhop welcomed him back and conducted him up to his preferred suite.

He tipped the man $10, kicked off his shoes and fell back onto the king-sized bed, releasing a relaxing breath. He looked forward to making a presentation to the Board of KZW the next morning. He felt well prepared. Jaimie, who was a figurehead non-executive Chairman for London and therefore not much involved in this worldwide process, had told him,

"You are one of three candidates under consideration. I can't say who the others are. It wouldn't be fair, besides, they'd think I told you. I will say this, there's one internal candidate."

"Well Jaimie, I've decided I can do this job and importantly could learn from seizing the challenge. I'm going for it. We will have to see."

As usual, he spent a couple of late-night hours going over his PowerPoint presentation and honing its accompanying monologue to perfection. At Kendrick, he had taught new intakes how to convince clients to action and had all the dos and don'ts of presentations off pat. His slides were light on words so as not to distract the viewers from the powerful illustrations on the screen. These were simple, clear and relevant. There were meaningful graphics. Dramatic and memorable photographs were used, with an occasional pertinent cartoon to lighten proceedings.

* * *

Next morning, Alex arrived early at the University Club of Chicago, where the KZW Board was to review the candidates. He noted the Neo-Gothic public rooms and the stained-glass windows. It's a Disneyland version of an Oxford College, built several centuries too late.

An obsequious porter ushered him up to the designated meeting room. It had dark wood paneling and a shiny Boardroom table. Green leather blotters lay in front of the reproduction Hepplewhite chairs.

Surprised at his intrusion, a couple of waiters were setting up for the meeting. This included preparing the coffee and a light buffet breakfast for the Board. He satisfied himself that he could stand facing the Board, without obscuring anyone's view of the screen and with a spotlight on his face. The show worked well on the equipment provided. Then he withdrew to the library to browse the papers and journals. This helped him relax, prior to his slot at 11:30 am. His request to go last had been granted. He wanted the Board to forget details from earlier pitches and to remember his, when they held their private discussions.

* * *

About an hour after Alex had left, the first Board members started to trickle in. As usual, there were exaggerated greetings, effusive handshakes or hugs and kisses. They made a bee-line for the coffee and food. All the serious horse-trading and lobbying was already complete. Knowing looks passed between those who had already agreed courses of action and preferred candidates.

Alice Contessa-Brecht made her traditional stately and somewhat late entrance, looking regally to the men on her left and right as she entered. Her demeanor was as though entering the court of the King of France. In a series of prior phone calls and meetings she had teased out the desires and objectives of each Board member. I'll hold my counsel and ensure that I get my way right at the end. She took a seat to the right of the Chairman. He always sat at the far end of the table facing the screen.

Jack saw through her false smile, as she patted his arm. Their mutual hatred almost crackled with electricity. She regarded him with a baleful eye, weighing the prospects that he might have a heart attack or a stroke if she riled him enough. Disappointed, she did not think it likely.

Alice often joked nastily with Jack's enemies about his auditing background.

"Ee is not even a bean counter. Ee merely checks that those oo do that get the numbers right."

He had won his position as Chairman in competition with Alice the previous year. No one liked him, partly because he claimed superior knowledge and experience of Board conduct. This was based on a little reading and his directorships with tiny companies. Despite this, many saw him as the lesser of two evils. Alice might be the Queen of Hell.

The Latin American and Asian Board members had adopted the mantra, "We are a US firm so we must have a US Chairman." The US partners did not trust each other, but anyone from the US was better than a foreigner. The Europeans were intent on preventing their neighbor, Alice, getting the job, either from jealousy or due to past resentments. She was the kind of accomplished and powerful woman that threatened their sense of masculinity.

Most Board members had specific backing from other partners from their regions. That was how they stayed elected to the Board.

Alice mentally ticked off the interests of those around the room. She had already thwarted Jack's ambitions to combine the Chairman's role with that of CEO at the last meeting. It had been easy to recruit the non-US partners to the line that good corporate governance required the separation of powers at this level.

Only in the US were great corporations dominated by combined CEOs and Chairmen. All the business schools and governance gurus were against it. She mused, Jack is still fuming about his defeat. Ee will be determined to win today. He will either want a weak CEO, so that he can dominate the man, or for us to fail to make an appointment. Then ee will be forced to step in, combining the role with that of Chairman. He has another think coming. Puffed up old fool. He thinks his previous partnership in accounting qualifies him. They are ten to the euro, score checkers. Unfortunately, 'is cronies, three other US directors will support 'im. Each owes 'im for past favors.

She switched her eyes to the director who was head of the San Francisco Office. Her spy in the Headquarters team told her he was screwing the internal candidate, John, the head of KZW's marketing. She therefore knew what he wanted and exactly how to block it.

Moving on, she saw Bob from Hong Kong. He is a man to watch. I never know what ee is up to. The Sydney and London senior partners were sitting close together and exchanging looks. Her information was that they favored Alex, because of his public profile and impressions they had formed from meeting him. Also, he had relevant experience from their regions.

All the Latin Americans were delighted to have the prospect of a fluent Spanish speaker in Alex. They had pressed the director from Chile to support him. Alice smiled inwardly. What would they say if zey discover Alex helped win the war for the Malvinas against Argentina? These nations squabble amongst themselves, yet they will support any Latino Soccer Club against outside teams.

The others had tried to discover Alice's preferences, but she had reserved her position. That will give me ze best chance to get what I want. When London tried to persuade me of the eternal solidarity between Britain and France, it was deliciously *drôle*. Quelle folie!

* * *

The Chairman asked that the first candidate be called in. The mouse-like Corporate Secretary scuttled out of the door to fetch him. The Chairman treated him as his personal servant. The man lived in constant fear of losing his pension.

The internal option, the Marketing Director from the Chicago headquarters, diffidently sidled though the half-open door. His brow sweated as he nervously looked around the room. The US directors gave him encouraging smiles, especially his lover, the senatorial director from San Francisco. The Chairman waved a welcoming arm towards the top of the table by the screen. Jack really wanted this guy. He was weak and would do his bidding. It would also guarantee the support of the San Francisco partners at the next election. Alice graciously smiled at the candidate, while watching the others like a hawk.

Encouraged, the candidate began his pitch for the job.

"Well, er good morning. All of you know me, er and I know this business. Er, I guess those are my great strengths. I've been asked to share my ideas of er how I'd do this job and so I've made a few PowerPoint slides."

He smiled weakly, blocking the view of half the audience from the screen.

"Er, you've had a few presentations from me at conferences in the past."

He turned his back on the directors to read each line of the too many on each slide. Flustered, he stumbled on. The London partner rolled his eyes. The director from Sydney did not hold back.

"Streuth John, if you'd just step away from the screen, we could all see what you're talkin' about. If all you're going to do is read it, we can do that ourselves."

Flustered, John shuffled to one side, desperately trying to see his lines.

"Oh! Sorry. Er, is that better?"

The Chairman charged in swiftly to his support.

"That's fine John, just relax and carry on."

As he spoke, John edged gradually down the side of the table, so he could read the slides more comfortably. Now he was speaking to the backs of half the Board. He warmed to his task. The gist of his pitch was that he would do his best to follow the instructions of the Chairman and the other directors. At the end the Chairman remarked,

"Well done John. That was really excellent."

Then, looking for support from his backers,

"Does anyone have any questions for John?"

San Francisco raised a hand. He asked why John felt inside experience was useful. John shared that there were many partners in the firm and they all had different ideas and needs. It had taken him years to understand them all.

Preening himself, Chile asked how John would address the specific problems of Latin America, especially

Brazil. It had a much bigger economy than Chile, but only half the size of the KZW business in his own country. John told him that he would spend time at regional meetings with the Latin American partners and then carry out their wishes.

John left the room feeling confidently warm. Some of the directors exchanged meaningful looks of disgust at his weakness as a candidate.

They broke off for coffee.

* * *

Half an hour later they reconvened. The second candidate was a senior partner from another executive search firm. In recent years, it had comprehensively outcompeted KZW. The Chairman called the meeting to order and asked that he begin. Supremely confident, he chose not to use any visual aids.

Alice watched him with amusement. Well at least zis one looks the part, $2,000 suit, suave and uses himself as ze best visual aid. Like many senior 'edhunters 'e is very tall and 'andsome, with the required iron grey hair. And ee is from zee US, most important for many 'ere.

The Chairman knew him from conferences, the industry's trade association and shootouts with his firm. He was worried that if he let this man win, he would sideline the Chair and pretty well take over.

The way the man criticized KZW during his pitch was entirely fair. It was not a great way to convince those with pride in their firm or delusions as to KZW's relative ranking. Alice judged that he was losing the Europeans, the Asia Pacific directors and of course both San Francisco and the Chairman.

When questioned as to how he would change things, his response lost him many points.

"Well, I'd take an inventory of all our professionals and check their performance against what I know can be done in that location from my former firm. Then, where necessary, we'll get rid of the dead wood. Fortunately, there are many in my old firm who I can persuade to come across."

Noticing the concern for their own jobs that this raised around the table, the German Deputy Chairman chimed in.

"Could you tell us why you separated from your former firm?"

The answer was already known. He had been fired after losing numerous fights for power in the Board. He put on a poker face and spouted the usual cover story about needing new challenges.

* * *

At 11:20 am Alex sipped a coffee in the area outside the room, fastening the middle button of his Jacket and straightening his tie. Must look the part. The last candidate caste him a confident glance as he left. Alex smiled back. His adrenaline was rising. It always did. It kept him at the top of his game.

Moments later, the Corporate Secretary opened the door and deferentially beckoned him in. Alex strode purposefully into the room. He shook hands with the Chairman, gave a cheery greeting to the others, acknowledging each in turn. His world tour of KZW was paying dividends. Assuredly, he took his chosen position by the side of the screen.

Jack welcomed him formally and asked him to present how he saw things and why they might select him.

Alex began with the screen blanked out. He liked the audience to look at him and only at the screen when he needed to lock an idea into their heads with a compelling picture.

"As you all know, I have been around the world, meeting your good selves and your senior colleagues. Thank you for your hospitality and most of all for sharing your views and ideas as to the strengths and improvement opportunities for this great firm. Much of what I am about to say, is based on what you and your colleagues shared with me on my visit to seventeen offices of KZW."

He went on to outline the issues they had raised. This received nods of approval from those who had made or agreed with his points.

The Chairman shifted uncomfortably in his seat as Alex showed slides with new information that the Board did not possess. They charted average billings per partner at leading rivals. KZW had relatively weak positioning in the growth economies and industries. KZW's relative performance in the US was abysmal. The Chairman went red in the face.

Other analysis indicated that change was essential, if the firm was to survive. He demonstrated how comparatively little KZW spent on its branding and marketing. He shared the results of a poll on brand recognition of leading search firms. KZW was hardly thought of. A few older respondents remembered it as being a formerly solid firm.

The San Francisco partner was floundering under the barrage of data that showed his candidate in a bad light.

"Where did you get this?"

"Oh, I asked one of my former researchers at Kendrick to knock it out as a favor. I did not tell her why. As you can see, that last slide was given to her by a competitor who had paid for the research."

Jack leapt on the point.

"Aha industrial espionage!"

"Oh no Mr. Chairman, just normal research."

Alice clapped her hands and exclaimed delightedly.

"Bravo Monsieur! Bravo!"

Others gave looks of approval. Sensing the majority view, Jack harrumphed. He shrank a little in his chair and glowered at Alex in silence.

Alex answered subsequent questions with aplomb. He left them with some thoughts.

"It is the eleventh hour for the survival of this business. We need to develop a common vision, invest in rebuilding the brand and eliminate or replace weak leaders and offices around the world. If we do this, the firm can reclaim its place as the leader in the Executive Search Industry.

The Chairman asked the last question,

"How long would that take?"

"It will be a two-year process to set the firm on the road to recovery. In my experience, if you cannot agree and action the necessary changes in that time, you never will. The analysis of this firm tells us that with your help, I can save and revitalize KZW. You have some great people. I have the skills and experience to release the potential and to make your firm great again.

"I ask only that you unanimously choose me. Only with a unified purpose and complete commitment from the Board can greatness be achieved. Without that, you are doomed to inevitable decline and eclipse."

After his goodbyes, Alex left. The Chairman was relieved and looked it. He proposed a break for lunch. Gloatingly he thought that there was no way in hell he was going to make it the unanimous vote Alex wanted. Enough of the others would surely feel the same. His ultimate goal of combining the CEO and Chairmanship felt within his grasp.

* * *

The director from San Francisco moved away from the buffet. Skillfully, the Contessa cut him out of the herd. She whispered softly, so he had to lean towards her to hear.

"You know I admire your work. I 'ave nussing against gay people either. But I 'ave to tell you that our head of marketing cannot do the CEO job and be your lover at the same time. If you support him, I will 'ave to explain why I do not. You know well that our Latin American friends are very prejudiced in zis matter. Your wife and kids would be sure to 'ear about it.

"I can keep zis quiet and will make sure he keeps is job in marketing.

In return and before we reconvene, you need to tell your American supporters that you 'ave changed your mind. I will explain to Jack myself, without giving him the real reason. Deal?"

Furious and worried, the director pursed his lips and wrinkled his brow. What would his wife and kids say or the elders in his Presbyterian church, if his secret life was made public?

"You really are a piece of work, Alice."

She smiled sweetly at him. Her menacing silence let his internal pressure build. His heart beat rapidly. His palms were sweating. For a moment, he considered blustering it out. He could deny everything. Then he deflated. She must have some evidence. Through gritted teeth he agreed.

"Deal."

She had no intention of warning the Chairman or retaining the failed marketing head. She did alert the Latin American director, betraying her word and whispering her suspicions. She had to be sure of him.

* * *

Confidently Chairman Jack reopened the meeting.

"Well perhaps we should start by eliminating a candidate, if we can. Then it's down to the other two. As Alex is not from our industry, I cannot support him. He demanded unanimity, therefore he is out."

Looking meaningfully to his US directors he said,

"How many agree?"

To his astonishment, they looked shifty. No one supported him.

Looking cross, the Chilean erupted.

"That is not fair. We need to discuss all the candidates and see if we can reach agreement."

Reluctantly, the Chairman sought another way to his chosen solution.

"Very well, in my view our competitor candidate was arrogant and disrespectful of us and our great firm. He was fired from his old firm for good reasons. He wants to rebuild his own firm without our key people. He is a threat to all of us."

Receiving nods all round, he asked,

"Does anyone support him?"

No one did. Therefore, he was eliminated. Sensing victory moving closer, Jack moved to his preferred choice.

"We have our internal candidate, John. He is always helpful and friendly. He knows all of us. We know him. He understands our industry. He listens to us. Jack turned to his ally from San Francisco.

"Do you want to speak in his favor?"

Refusing to meet the Chairman's eyes and looking shiftily down at the table, he mumbled a response.

"Well, as many of you know, I like John. I thought he was a good candidate, but as Alex pointed out, many of our problems are due to a lack of marketing success. Also, maybe he should have been the one showing us the competitive data. I just think he is too weak a man for the task. I support Alex."

Bob showed his Tiger's smile. His eyes watched Jack closely.

Furious and surprised, Jack raised his voice.

"Well that's it then. As Alex demanded unanimity and I will vote against him, we have no suitable candidate. We will have to look again. Meantime, I will have to step into the CEO role until we find someone else."

The Contessa, hissed menacingly. Startled, all eyes looked to her.

"Wait a moment. Zere is another way to get unanimity. If Jack cannot support an excellent candidate, then maybe we should have a vote of confidence in 'is Chairmanship? You might have to choose Jack."

The Tiger from Hong Kong pounced.

"Yes Jack, there is no shame in retiring at your age."

Incandescent and again coloring red, Jack recoiled. He looked desperately to the other Americans for support. He saw none. Rapidly weighing his options, he caved in.

"Well if you feel like that, perhaps I've been a bit hasty. I will support Alex."

The vote was unanimous.

With a triumphant look, Alice savored her victory.

"Well given Jack's views, we should let our Deputy Chairman give Alex ze good news and negotiate his deal."

Jack looked daggers at her, seeing his last chance to nix the deal slipping away.

CHAPTER EIGHTEEN

Seizing the Day

"Nothing is harder to deal with, more dangerous to undertake, or riskier to success than to lead in establishing a new order of things."

Niccolo Machiavelli

After the Board vote. Alex was fired up. *Most of the partners I've met want change. The unanimous Board vote I asked for gives me the mandate I need to make that happen.* Alex's subsequent meeting with the German Deputy Chairman further boosted his confidence.

"You could find better headquarters premises, if zey do not cost more.

Moving zem away from Jack's search office and his interference would be a good sing. It will stop him getting tales from your underlings."

The Deputy Chairman was surprised when Alex refused the salary he was offered.

"Look, pay me a dollar a year. The $300,000 you offer will do for my travel expenses. I'd like to be an equal partner in the firm, just the same as the office leaders. I will make money from the improvement of the stock value. I want to be on the same footing as the other partners."

"Vy do you need to travel so much?"

"We need to bring every office along with the change program. Some offices will have to be closed. For others, we have to find new leaders. In addition, I intend to work hard at promoting our firm in the major countries. That will mean TV appearances and attending CEO conferences."

"That's a good idea, but be careful. "Ze local leaders see that as zeir job."

"Not to worry, I will include them in this. Besides, if they had been doing their job, it would already be happening. KZW would be a better-known brand.

"There's one other thing, I need to hire a good assistant. I'm not meaning a secretary. There's a Danish fellow I worked with at Goldring. He has a Harvard MBA and is brilliant in change management. His name is Mads Petersen. Here's his résumé."

* * *

A month later, Alex sat in the newly rented headquarters office of KZW. He had found a decent place in a less fashionable suburb of Chicago. It was nothing like the prestigious office space used by Goldring or even Kendrick. He liked it that way. A Spartan style would go down well with the partners. They resented every penny spent by the center. It also put his new team in a lean and mean mode. He had sold the idea to the Board by pointing out that clients met in the search offices, so there was no point in keeping HQ staff in luxury surroundings.

Jack had been furious, but was outvoted once more. The only support Jack received was from the San Francisco director. He was cross that Alex had fired his friend the marketing head. He could do little about the fait accompli, especially as the man had been given a substantial severance package and already signed the separation agreement.

* * *

Alex reviewed progress with Mads Petersen. He liked working with Mads. His razor-sharp intellect often brought new insights and ideas. Besides conversation sometimes strayed to their common interest in Buddhism, quantum mechanics and many other subjects.

Things were moving along at pace. They had a list of offices to be eliminated in markets that had proved to be non-viable. In Pakistan, the economy was in the tank. There were few inward investors from the developed world used to using executive search. Large local firms tended to appoint family members or those with connections to the corrupt government or the military. Venezuela had become another wrecking yard for all advisory firms. Alex spurred his Board into closing twenty such offices, despite opposition from Jack, who relied on votes from the partners there.

The worst performing or retirement-age partners elsewhere were to be "counseled out" or given honorary titles such as "Director Emeritus." In his time at Kendrick, Alex had learned the subtleties of putting senior people out to grass with reduced pain. He had found that a title with respect and recognition was more important than financial rewards. This was especially true for people who insisted on working past the age when their acuity was in decline. It was vital to get such people out of the way. It allowed new leaders the space to develop.

The current KZW organization has become sclerotic with oldsters clogging the decision processes. Chairman Jack is a prime example. His Chicago office has seen a procession of good hires. They left, because he insists on making all the decisions himself. He's jealous of other's success and steals their opportunities. This was a common issue in other KZW offices too.

In neglected, but important markets there were to be thirty new operations. This was change on a grand scale. The brakes that the Board put on slowed progress. Alex and Mads were increasingly frustrated.

On his travels, Alex discovered other aberrant activities.

* * *

During his further office visits, he encountered strange and unprofessional ways for selecting candidates to present to clients.

In Osaka, he was having dinner with the KZW office head. After sharing several flasks of warm Saki, Alex asked,

"How did you select your number two."

The answer both fascinated and appalled him.

"Well, of course we used numerology. Then we gave him the blood test."

Alex kept a serious face. *I mustn't laugh. He would never forgive me for his loss of face.* He struggled with the image of reaching across an interview desk, seizing a startled candidate's arm, ramming in a needle and extracting a blood sample.

He knew that, in much of Asia, clients believed in numerology, astrology and other such unscientific evidence of candidate suitability. Because it was the local culture, professional businesses had to accept and adopt these and other practices as a sham. He recalled Kendrick calling in the Feng Shui man to nail copper rods under a desk he was using in Singapore. It was explained that if he had not allowed this, staff would not want to work with him. He had also witnessed a Lion Dance to bless a new Shanghai office at Goldring. He understood the need to adapt to local cultures and superstitions. He believed that beneath that respect and façade, strictly professional and globally standardized methodologies were vital.

I can't believe that some in the KZW offices actually believe in this stuff. He later discovered that in the case mentioned, blood was swirled in a porcelain cup by a shaman. He would evaluate the results in a similar way to a Rorschach test or as fortunetellers read tea leaves.

Subsequently, Alex found that such superstitious practices were not confined to Asia. A junior in the Munich office confided mistrust in his Geschäftsführer. This general manager was wont to suspend a magic stone on a cord over a candidate's photograph. If it became excited and swung wildly, that was the chosen one. Furthermore, the leader took his team up to the ley lines in the nearby Alps on weekends. This was to seek the earth's support in winning business. He also claimed to spot auras around the best executives.

The biggest surprise was the Contessa's disclosure that the French and Belgian offices really believed in Graphology to choose candidates. Alex showed her the evidence that using handwriting samples was no better way to pick candidates than random selection. She would not have it and became cross.

"It iz what we do and it works. Leave us alone. You will see."

* * *

In another instance, Alex had had to cover up a case where a KZW candidate had been using company funds to fund a sex addiction, complete with online porn, hookers, orgies and cocaine. When he investigated the case, he found that this could have been avoided by interviewing past work colleagues. The man had been fired twice for such behavior. Companies preferred to bury such skeletons in order to avoid reputational damage. They gave great references to bad employees. *KZW should have done better.*

To deal with all this Alex and Mads hired specialist trainers. They established a program for behavioral interviewing. Candidates were to be treated the same all over the world. That is what the big multinational corporations needed. Leaders would be evaluated: on their verified performance, by matching their management behavior to the needs of the client, and by rigorous background checking.

* * *

Mads raised important issues with Alex.

"What would we do in our former firm, if KZW sought our advice?"

"We'd consider moves such as switching the location of the corporation's HQ to a large growth market. We'd evaluate selling out to a competitor or investor better placed to squeeze value from the business, or we could find an alliance with or acquire a firm that could bring superior technology, branding or management."

These ideas were similar to those of Bob, the Hong Kong Tiger. They financially modeled and discussed these scenarios late into the nights. They began to examine some of them in depth. The location in Chicago was especially irksome. The costs of space and employment were high.

They shared their thinking with the strategy committee from the Board. Jack nearly had an apoplectic fit, but the majority agreed that all options should be considered.

The Contessa's eyes had lit up during the presentation. *Ah, now I can bring an opportunity that will allow me to take over.*

* * *

A few days after that Board meeting, Alice called for a special, virtual Board meeting using the KZW video link. She revealed an opportunity to bring in a large French investor to recapitalize and develop the firm.

"Every shareholder could make millions of dollars from zis. Even better, partners will stay in control of ze offices and KZW could become ze number one in our industry."

The Board agreed that Alice should work with Alex to evaluate this. It made sense, as she had the contact.

* * *

Alex was invited to a dinner at Alice's Paris apartment. He was a little nervous that she had designs on his body. *Could I resist? She's incredibly attractive. I'll keep things professional and restrict the alcohol.* He was relieved when a handsome butler answered the door.

Alice made her usual spectacular entrance. She was ravishing, swathed in a long silk dress. It clung to her buttocks and had a plunging neckline. A large emerald glittered with the same colour as her eyes. It hung on a gold chain, drawing his eyes in the direction they were eager to go. She hugged him, kissing him three times on the cheeks. That overpowering scent was stronger than last time.

"Welcome Mon Cheri. Zis is how we French greet friends."

She felt him stiffen slightly in her grasp thinking. *Too late mon brave, you are already snared in my web.*

He felt safer when a pretty girl, assisted the butler in serving drinks. He had a small whisky and planned to have only one glass of wine with dinner. When they were seated Alice's voice became husky.

"You must try zis wine. Eet is Chateau Laffite 45. A wonderful and rare vintage."

* * *

Alex awoke to the caress of silk sheets, feeling the warmth, accompanied by the sweet smell of the woman pressed against him. He felt wonderfully exhausted, but was still aroused. He struggled to remember the evening, as he opened one eye. *Jesus it's the maid. What have I done? Alice must have put something in the wine.*

Leaving the girl asleep, he noticed the faint smell of Alice's mysterious perfume on his arm. *This gets worse. Will she blackmail me, or was she just having fun?* Quickly, he showered, discovering bloody scratch marks scored across his back. Rapidly donning yesterday's clothes, he planned to slip out of the house without being noticed.

He was gingerly tiptoeing through the salon, when he noticed Alice tucking into breakfast in the dining room. She looked right at him, with a wicked smile. Her eyes twinkled.

"We know how to entertain in Paris, Non?"

Reluctantly, he was forced to be phlegmatic.

"I slept well thank you. Do you mind if I join you?"

As they ate, Alice handed him two pages of paper across the table. It was in French, but was easy to translate. "Heads of Agreement between KZW and Finance de Paris SA." He knew this was a subsidiary of one of the largest French banques d'affaires, or investment houses.

What he read appalled him. Alice had taken things much further than she had disclosed to the KZW Board. The heads of agreement were detailed and comprehensive.

1. Alice Contessa-Brecht will be the Chairman of a new company X.

2. X will control the shares of KZW.

3. Finance de Paris will receive 51% of X for $250 million Euros and have four Board seats.

4. Alex McDonald will be the Directeur General of the new company.

5. ....

Alex looked up at Alice.

"This has gone much further than you led us to understand."

"Zere is no point in wasting time Alex. We have a meeting wiz our buyer at 3:00 pm today."

She smirked.

"You may wish to go back to your 'otel and change."

* * *

In his hotel room, Alex sat for a few moments considering his position. He reached some firm conclusions. *I will do what is right for KZW. If this offer is to be considered, it has to be fully disclosed to the Board. In the case of an unsolicited offer to buy a firm, good strategy dictates that we seek the best partners for KZW and therefore seek other buyers. Those with a better fit could add more value and therefore pay more. Only after such an analysis should Finance de Paris be considered.*

It seems likely that Alice might try to blackmail me to recommend this deal. In that case, I would have to resign and state my reasons. The threat of that may deter her. If not, I will take the consequences.

OK that is the plan, now how do I add clever tactics to get through this?

* * *

Alex met Alice in the waiting area of Finance de Paris's discrete offices. The great and the good liked anonymity when discussing big deals. She asked,

"How do you want to play this Alex?"

"Well we should explore the offer further of course and then report back to the Board."

"Ah, I knew you would be sensible. Eet is a good deal and zere are other possibilities."

Two well-dressed men in dark suits greeted them as they entered a meeting room. Alex noted from the hugs and kisses that the leader seemed to know Alice very well indeed.

From his days as a banker, Alex remembered that such meetings were best begun by seeking possible connections on past deals and with other bankers that both parties knew. If there were connections, it established the seriousness of the other party. Also, their trustworthiness could be explored with the mutual acquaintances. Naturally, the French financiers knew people in both Goldring and Kendrick. They seemed comfortable with Alex.

The discussion was amiable. Alex focused on what advantages being owned by a French finance house would bring to KZW. Alice nodded as the boss explained the benefits.

"Of course, we 'ave fabulous connections in our government as well as in the higher echelons of all ze large

French corporations. Our friends and influence reach to all former French colonies and to our trading partners across the world."

Alex smiled amiably, keeping his thoughts to himself. *This is all too focused on France for a global firm. Alice's business would benefit most. She is supposed to already deal with all the key players in France.*

The Financier continued,

"Alice believes zat with the money we provide we can build many advantages for KZW: better marketing, recruitment of top performers, buying competitors, and investing in improved IT."

Alex agreed. He noticed Alice relaxing as he did so.

"Well we certainly need to do most, if not all of those things."

The conversation went on for another hour. They agreed to renew contact when Alex had advised the KZW Board of the offer. Afterward, Alice invited Alex back to her place for drinks. Alex laughed.

"Ha, thanks, but after last night I would feel safer in a café."

"Oh, but it was so much fun. We French do not take such things so seriously."

* * *

They sat in a booth in a nearby bistro sipping glasses of red wine. Alice leaned towards him conspiratorially. Then spoke to him with increasing excitement.

"Now here is ze really interesting sing. Our finance friends sink it would be a good idea to insert another company between themselves and X company. Zey want you and I to own 49% of that company, let us call it Y company. Zat would mean that we and Finance de Paris, would have complete control over KZW, but ze current partners would think they still own 49% because of X company. You would have to put in say 100 million Euros for your share of Y company. We could then ensure zat all ze profits flow to ze owners of Y company. Magnifique! Non?"

Appalled at such a corrupt deal, Alex decided to keep his powder dry. He pretended to be interested. They agreed to speak before the Board meeting. He finished by saying,

"Alice, the Chairman would never agree to all this. He doesn't want change."

"Do not worry about 'im. Ee will not be an obstacle."

Alex wondered what blackmail opportunities Alice might have on Jack. Still, he just wanted to get back to the Chicago and to discuss the whole thing with Mads. He would share everything.

CHAPTER NINETEEN

Coup de Main

"In the short space of an hour comes rapid death or joyful victory."

Horace

In an off-site meeting room in Chicago, Alex explained the whole sorry saga of his French visit to Mads. He left nothing out. Mads asked whether Alex's position was weakened by the danger of revelations from his night at Alice's apartment. It clearly was. They went on to develop a strategy to pre-empt the danger of that. In the middle of the discussion, Alex's cell phone buzzed.

It made him anxious. He had instructed his office to contact him only in emergencies. He listened to the message. Looking shocked, he turned to Mads.

"Jack's dead! It was a hit and run, as he was going to his office."

Alex's head was whirling with worries and ideas. OK, it could have been an accident. Maybe the mysterious killer of the Goldring Chairman with the car bomb is dogging my footsteps. No. Why would anyone do that? Except that somehow, I was implicated in that. British Intelligence pulled me in for questioning. Or maybe this is what Alice meant when she told me Jack would not be a problem. Bloody hell!

Abandoning their meeting, Jack and Mads headed back to their office. The next Board event was going to be doubly interesting.

* * *

Alex and Mads spent the days before the meeting choreographing Alex's moves on the key agenda points very carefully. Alex spent a lot of time by phone with those he felt he could trust. It was going to be tricky.

The Corporate Statutes stated:

"In the case of a Chairman vacancy, the Deputy Chairman shall replace him, until an election for a new Chairman takes place...

"This should be within a month of the previous Chairman's departure...

"The Board will elect its preferred candidate...

"Following this and within a week there should be a vote of all partners...

The Chairman elect should then receive a simple majority of those voting to be the winner."

They decided that the best course of action was to keep Alice happy.

Alex would also disclose the whole sorry saga to the Deputy Chairman.

* * *

Jack's, death caused a flurry of emails and phone calls between other KZW partners. They loved such opportunities to gossip about colleagues, rivals and enemies within the firm. The choices for next Chairman were the main topic.

* * *

There were discrete communications between the FBI and the British clandestine services MI5 and MI6. Another death of someone closely connected to Alex seemed a more than unlikely coincidence. All the police files were shared between them. When the FBI read various KZW emails, they soon discovered that Alex was one of those who found Jack a major obstacle to his plans. They also sought connections that might lead to the motorcycle bomber of the Goldring Chairman in Connecticut.

Maria Ramirez was undercover in Uzbekistan for a Russian client, when her news service relayed the story about Jack. She was intrigued at the professionalism of the hit, if that was what it was. Fingering the scar on her face, she vowed to catch up with Alex when the occasion arose. She set her mouth in a grim smile. They still had unfinished business. Meanwhile, let him squirm.

* * *

In her Paris apartment, Alice was watching a video file on her computer. Her back arched in the chair, remembering the pleasure she had enjoyed in making it. The clip clearly showed Alex, eyes crazed with passion and drugs. She was clawing deep scratches on his back as he thrust into her. He was roaring with ecstasy like a bull.

With the threat of the recording hanging over him, Alex had readily agreed to her plan of action. She refreshed her memory of her hold over other Board members with five other files. Few had been as much fun as the first one. With these votes, she was certain of her election as Chairman.

* * *

The KZW Board meeting was held in the University Club of Chicago. They used the same room in which Alex had been chosen as CEO. As the Board members filed in, some wore black ties and dark suits. Alex noted that Alice was wearing a charcoal silk dress and jet jewelry. She had donned a sober demeanor for the occasion. Conversation was muted and the atmosphere somber as they took their places.

The Deputy Chairman coughed. Everyone paid attention.

"As you know, I am acting as Chairman, until vee haf another one. Vee have sree items on zee agenda. First is to record a vote of sanks to Jack for his years of service to zis firm."

Many of them had loathed Jack. No one had actually liked him. However, after a few words of false praise from one or two, the motion was proposed by Alice and seconded by Bob, the Hong Kong Tiger. It was unanimously approved.

"Next, vee need to recommend the Board's choice for a new Chairman. Who vould like to stand for this position? Just to be clear, I vill not be doing so."

The Director from San Francisco leaned forward in his seat to intervene excitedly.

"Mr. Deputy Chairman, I'd like to raise a point of order. It wouldn't be right for our CEO to be present or vote on this matter. He'd be voting for his own boss."

Alex relaxed in his chair. This issue had been anticipated. The Deputy Chairman turned to the Corporate Secretary to pronounce on the rules. He responded and quoted from documents he had to hand.

"Mr. McDonald's contract specifically states that, "He will be a full director of the Board of KZW with the same privileges and voting rights on all issues as other directors." We also have here the relevant parts of our statutes. "The full Board, present in person, should choose a new Chairman, either from among themselves or from other members of the partnership. A majority of all Board members voting is required."

San Francisco looked crestfallen. The Deputy Chairman waited for people to nominate themselves. By pre-arrangement with Alex, the director from London spoke.

"I think Alex should take the job, he is doing well and has the confidence of all of us."

Rival candidates and their supporters were startled. Some were about to protest. Alex intervened. His purpose in being proposed was for the Board to understand that he was not motivated by power, but by the wellbeing of KZW.

"Thank you for your confidence in me, but I will not be standing. Good corporate governance requires the separation of the Chair and the CEO. The US is somewhat behind in the acceptance of this. Combination concentrates too much power in one person. Besides managing Board affairs and the business of the company is too much for one person. My plate is full with our change program."

Alice smiled with approval. There were one or two looks of relief. Alice and Bob, both self-nominated for the Chairmanship, so did the Director from Sydney, Joe Toohey. The three candidates each explained why they should be the Chairman.

* * *

Progress on the investigation of Jack's death was discussed in a conference call between the FBI case officer in Chicago and the two British intelligence agencies. Judd of MI6 and Roberts of MI5 were in the same room in London.

"I'm sorry gentlemen, but we have nothing new to report from here in the US. As we already shared, if it was a hit, it was so well executed that there is no conclusive evidence. Like you, we are very suspicious of the trail of bodies following Alex McDonald around the world. He had motives in every case, except for his wife. Even there, who knows what marital stresses there are behind closed doors? He has concrete alibis in every case. If he is involved, he must have one or more accomplices."

Judd looked at Roberts and raised his beetle brows questioningly. Roberts leaned towards their speaker phone.

"We share your suspicions. There is another possibility. Maybe someone has it in for McDonald, and is attempting to harm him or frame him."

The answer from Chicago was incredulous.

"Crap! There's been no evidence that anyone is seeking to implicate McDonald in this instance. We want to put a watch on McDonald and get further warrants to record all his communications."

"Judd here, strictly between us, we've already done that. McDonald seemed genuinely surprised by Jack's death. Our recordings suggest that he suspects a French party. The lady has something on him and may be blackmailing him. He could be laying this out for our benefit of course. He's very tricky. We trained him. If he's right though, this could be an unrelated case."

"Listen Judd. I'll ignore your illegal wiretapping here in the US, as long as you share what you have. We'll keep in touch on this."

* * *

Alice strolled confidently from the room. She bestowed haughty smiles left and right. While the Deputy Chairman and Corporate Secretary counted the votes, the others made small talk outside.

Five minutes later they were called back and took their seats. Alice expected to receive an immediate majority, removing the need for a second round. The Deputy Chairman announced,

"The votes were as Follows: 1 spoiled ballot. 2 for Joe Toohey; 4 for Alice Contessa-Bracht and 4 for Robert Lee-Soames. With your agreement, we will hold a second round and Joe Tooey will drop out."

Toohey, a happy go lucky fellow, seemed unconcerned.

"Well, you have to try. Maybe next time."

Alice was shocked and furious. Which sniveling little bastards were betraying her? She needed a break to remind her supposed supporters about the threat of her files.

"Might I suggest a coffee break so we can gather out thoughts?"

The Deputy Chairman answered her.

"No Alice. This should only take a few minutes. Let's go right ahead."

She seethed with anger, contenting herself with menacing looks to each of her supporters. Most of them flinched.

After the vote once again they filed out. On re-entering, the Chairman announced,

"We have a clear winner. The votes were: Alice Contessa-Brach 4 votes. Robert Lee-Soames 6 votes. Robert will go to the partnership vote as the Board's recommended candidate.

"Now let's take a coffee break. Then we can move on to other matters."

As others shook hands to congratulate a smiling Bob, Alice stormed out of the room. She scrutinized her face in the ladies' room mirror. She looked old. Her features were twisted with vexation and venom. Tears of frustration welled up in her eyes. Dabbing them with a tissue, they blazed back at her.

She gathered her thoughts. She could not reveal all the files she had on Board members. She had to be selective. She needed to know who had betrayed her. Then she would act. Meantime, that half-Chinese mongrel had better enjoy himself. He'll be dealt with later. She made running repairs with her makeup.

Back with the group, Alice scrutinized every face looking for traitors.

She watched intently as Alex spelt out the advantages of selling KZW to the French Finance House. Was he lacking enthusiasm? He seemed to support her, but she knew the motion would fail. Chairman Elect Bob, spoke against it. She proposed that the motion would be rejected to avoid loss of face. It was, by a unanimous show of hands.

Alice settled into her Air France first class seat. As the plane prepared to take-off for Paris, she sipped Champagne. She would have someone hack into all KZW's emails. That should reveal those who had stabbed her in the back. Meantime, she would enjoy planning for agonizing retribution for the guilty.

CHAPTER TWENTY

The Typhoon Arrives

"Courageous are those who see clearly what is in front of them, peril and danger equally, yet they advance to the challenge."

Pericles

Mads and Alex sat in a conference room in the Mandarin Hotel in Bangkok. They were planning Alex's presentation of progress to the annual KZW Asia/Pacific conference a week hence.

Alex especially liked this hotel. A short ride across the bustling Chao Phraya River in the hotel's private junk led to the hotel's famous Thai Cookery school. It served exquisite meals. From the window of his suite, he loved to watch the slender, high-prowed long-tail boats speeding by. Their roaring US V-8 car engines with unguarded propellers churned massive wakes. Unlucky passengers in nearby craft were sprayed with filthy river water. The lumbering bulk of barges carrying rice, gasoline and other goods ploughed up and down the river at a more leisurely pace.

Mads and Alex brainstormed items for the presentation. Each shouted out areas where progress and achievements had been made. Mads then scribbled an abbreviated headline on the whiteboard, for later consideration and expansion. The final key points would be woven into a script, sprinkled with illustrating data and PowerPoint images. Mads began. Alex alternated.

"20% growth this year and 25% compound growth since you took the helm."

"Good one-resulting from adding eight new offices that accounted for half of the increased revenue. The rest came from organic growth in our existing offices."

"Increase to 80% of name recognition of our brand among business leaders, from last year's 70%. This goes with an increase of repeat business by 20% and CEO level placements now up to 30% of all hires."

"Ok Mads. How about some infrastructure achievements, for example:

- Global data base of candidates, that tracks the performance of people in the roles we place them in.

- Roll out of the behavioral interview training and standardized approach to recruitment process.

Our team sweated blood to get those finished."

They continued long into the night over Singha beer and pizzas. The conversation moved on to threats to the firm and challenges for the future. The whiteboard was abandoned. Alex expounded,

"You know Mads; the worst issue we face is the dysfunctional culture of our so called entrepreneurial office heads."

"How do you mean?"

"For a start, most of them act like tin-pot dictators in their own territories. Few share decisions with other rainmakers in the office. Worse, if anyone starts being more successful than they are, they resent it. The combination of those two things drives the best people out. They move to other firms where they can become part of the leadership. That means that those remaining are ineffective yes-men. They have no succession planning because they cannot grow strong people."

"Yes, that's a problem Alex. Another aspect of local despotism is lack of compliance with world-wide initiatives. Clients want centralized data from us, to manage their international recruitment quality. These are seen as direct threats to our office heads' absolute power. A case in point is that multinationals want standard interview techniques, speed of delivery and central control. Our decentralized, structure sits ill with that."

"And Mads, the other aspect of their lust for local independence is that they battle with each other over who owns clients, how to share fees and everything else. They cheat one another and the overall firm. We've had just a couple of cases where they've been caught fiddling the books and diverting fees into private accounts, but I bet it's the tip of the iceberg. The worst of it is when they bring disputes to me and I make a ruling. It always leaves one side or both dissatisfied. As time passes, we're building resentment and an ever-increasing number of enemies. That'll bite us in the ass eventually.

"Desires for localism are the biggest strategic threat to our integration plans. Also, they're likely to lead to the Board getting rid of us at some point. Mads, you'd better be prepared for the day they walk in and fire us."

"What do we do if that looks likely boss?"

"We watch out for signs: shifty body language, conversations that end as we appear, traps laid for us to stumble into—that sort of thing."

* * *

At a discrete table in London's Special Forces Club, Roberts of MI5 speared a Brussels sprout with his fork. Judd was filling him in on the latest intelligence on the murder of the last Chairman of KZW.

"It seems that this French Contessa is a real Lady Macbeth. We have no admissions. On the other hand, our surveillance of her communications and computers revealed extremely kinky sex and criminal plots against several current KZW Board members, clients and French government ministers. She has links to organized crime. She's become the prime suspect. She wants to destroy our boy Alex too."

Finishing his mouthful of sprout, Roberts asked,

"Fair enough. Should we alert the FBI and warn Alex?"

"No, the FBI will go all territorial about our illegal wire taps. Let 'em find their own killer. Murderous Frenchies are not our concern either. As for Alex, he's been a pain in the arse ever since that Czech fiasco. Maybe our Contessa will deal with our problem there."

"Fine by me. Maybe the Contessa would make a great asset for MI6. Let me know if there is anything new. This lamb is really excellent."

* * *

Alex's presentation to the conference went exceptionally well. The hundred and fifty delegates were also proud of KZW's progress. They rose to their feet and applauded for a full minute. Alex noticed that Alice was not smiling. Her clapping lacked enthusiasm. Still, he felt he had the continued support of the firm behind him.

Mads reminded him,

"Well at least they seemed happy with the presentation. You achieved a 94% favorable vote at the director's election only nine months ago. That should keep the wolves away for a while."

* * *

Next day, Alex laid out his plans for the future to the Board. The directors seemed subdued. Maybe they were tired. He was confident as he left the room for them to go into executive session, in the meeting room.

As he opened the door, he noted a couple of hostile looks. He confided in Mads,

"I know this sounds like a moan, but Chief executives always worry about executive sessions. The discussions take place in my absence. They can review anything, from the strategy of the firm to my performance. It's like something out of Kafka's book, *The Trial*. They discuss things they can have little knowledge of. They can accuse me of anything and find me guilty without me knowing why I'm in trouble. Nor need they allow me to offer any defense."

"Sounds like a breach of natural justice."

"It's certainly that, if there is any natural justice. It's also the state of the art corporate governance. It works because CEO's can become too powerful and dominate proceedings. It's fine as long as there are no directors angling for the job of CEO. Then it is Kafkaesque. We have to live with it. You or I can be kicked out without ever knowing why.

"Some of the directors looked a bit shifty when I talked to them at the Board meeting. It was almost like they were, not interested in my report. There's something afoot. Maybe we should be worried. Still things are going well. They have no reason to shoot the captain when we are on course, with a fair wind behind us."

"What can we do?"

"Relax. No doubt we will get some feedback and questions later."

* * *

The new Chairman of KZW, Bob Lee-Soames, the Hong Kong Tiger, called the directors to order. His yellow eyes surveyed the room and he smiled. Alice had proposed a motion to fire Alex. Given Alex's outstanding performance both at the conference and in terms of results, he had widespread support. Lee-Soames did not expect the motion to pass. If it did, he would assume the CEO role temporarily. Then, he could persuade the partners to change the statutes to make it permanent. Either way he was happy. He opened the meeting.

"Alice I think you have something to say?"

"Thank you, Mr. Chairman. We need to dismiss Alex. Immediately."

"Dramatically waving a folder, she began handing copies of photographs around the table. There were gasps from those not already briefed.

"These photographs were sent to me anonymously. If I 'ave zem, so must others. Making no judgment about his morality, we cannot let 'im stay. The girl and man in zese pictures were my employees. Zat is an outrageous abuse of my 'ospitality. Both 'ave been fired."

These were pictures Alice had held back from Alex. She did not feature in the selection she had prepared for the Board. She knew that the homophobic directors from Spain and Chile would be especially shocked by the shot of a frenzied Alex being taken from behind by her chauffer, as Alex thrust into her maid simultaneously.

A couple of directors, who had received her hospitality in the past, noticed that the background was Alice's secret room. She had pictures of them too. They could hardly object to her subterfuge, lest they were revealed.

The Sydney Director asked,

"How's this going to look to the partners? He's popular and the results he's got us are spectacular."

Lee-Soames said they would leak rumors about Alex around the firm. Gossip would do the rest. Anyway, it would be a fait accompli. The motion to dismiss Alex was carried unanimously. They agreed to fire Mads too. Alice added a rider that Alex would be cheated out of his stock with some legal technicalities and Mads would not receive his expected bonus or any severance. They voted that the process would be discussed with lawyers in Chicago before executing the action. Alex was independently wealthy and well connected. He might vindictively reveal unpleasant truths about KZW.

Alice smiled triumphantly at Lee-Soames. *I'ave plans for you too Mr. Tiger.*

* * *

A year later, Chairman Lee-Soames died in suspicious circumstances at a KZW conference in Las Vegas. Alice Contessa de Brecht was elected as Chairman. Mads and Alex were initially on a list of suspects. Soon the investigators' focus fell on Alice. Finding no evidence after a year, the matter became a cold case file.

CHAPTER TWENTY-ONE

Struggling With Anger and Revenge

"May all beings be happy and secure, may they be happy-minded!

Whatever living beings there are—feeble or strong, long, stout or medium,

short, small or large, seen or unseen (ghosts, gods and hell-beings),

those dwelling far or near, those who are born or those who await rebirth,

may all beings, without exception be happy-minded."

Karaniya Metta Sutta from the Pali Canon

The Doi Tung Mountain rises nearly 5,000 feet in the northernmost province of

Chiang Rai, Thailand. As he waited for hours outside the heavy wooden gates of the remote monastery near its peak, Alex was tired and thirsty. A nervous member of the Akha Hilltribe had guided him on the dangerous climb, in exchange for the last of Alex's money. It included precipitous secret pathways through the jungle.

They had heard the crackle of gunfire and seen a tiger's spore, but had avoided contact. The nearby Golden Triangle on the borders of Myanmar, Laos and Thailand was ravaged by drug smugglers, the murderous Burmese Army and various Shan Warlords. Alex wanted a place where no one would follow. Now, as he sat in the dust, ever more desperate for water, and lumpy with vicious insect bites, he wondered if the gate would ever open.

At last, it swung open. A saffron-robed, shaven-headed monk looked at him and grunted in Thai.

"What you want? Go away."

Alex bowed his head and replied in broken Thai,

"I seek enlightenment."

The gate slammed. A heavy iron bar banged back into place. An hour later a different, taller monk, a Caucasian, appeared from behind him. He came from a hidden entrance. He had an Australian drawl.

"So, you're still here. Follow me."

An hour later, Alex had been fed and watered. He was led to see the Abbot. After a lengthy interrogation, during which Alex confessed his need to battle his immense anger, he was admitted. He spent the next four years inside the walls of the monastery and in contemplation along the adjacent forest pathways. He sometimes remembered how he had come to be there.

* * *

A month after KZW's Executive Board meeting in Thailand, Alex and Mads were back in Chicago working on plans to hire important rainmakers from competitors. Alex glanced at his e-mail.

"Hmm. The Chairman wants to meet me over breakfast at the Drake tomorrow. I didn't know he was in town. It's a long flight from Hong Kong. It must be something important."

"Maybe he wants to finally drive through the changes the Board keeps blocking?"

* * *

As he entered the Drake breakfast room, Alex spotted Bob Lee-Soames, the Hong Kong Tiger, at a corner table with a serious looking man he did not know. He smiled and waved. He received a cold golden-eyed stare in return. His stomach tightened with apprehension. The hairs on his neck erected.

He joined them at the table. Brushing aside his pleas-antries, Lee-Soames introduced the other man, a part-ner from a top Chicago law firm. As Alex ordered break-fast, they both looked grim. Lee-Soames got straight to the point.

"Alex, I have to tell you that the members of the Board have instructed me to require your immediate resigna-tion. Here is the separation agreement."

Winded, Alex gathered his thoughts, as he glanced through the simple two-page official letter. No reasons were given. He noticed a clause depriving him of his shares. Another paragraph required him not to commu-nicate with or recruit any member of the firm, nor to set up in the same industry. There was a place for his signature at the bottom.

"May I ask why? Also, I'd like to share this with my lawyer before I respond."

Lee-Soames shot back, unblinking yellow eyes fixed on Alex. As he spoke, the sober suited lawyer gave an occasional nod of agreement.

"Chicago is an 'at-will employer.' We need offer no explanations. We require a signature before we leave here. If not, you will simply be dismissed on the spot. Should you try to return to the office, you will be barred. Given your background, we have hired armed security. Your personal belongings will be sent on to your apartment. If you sign, we will give you good references, as it sets in out in letter."

Alex's heart and mind raced. He suppressed his natural urge to leap across the table and dispatch the smug, fat Chairman and thin dour lawyer. A knife lay by his plate. He figured he could slaughter them both in seconds, even without the weapon. He breathed deeply, calming down.

Seething inside, he replied, stony-faced and flinty-eyed.

"Well I'm not signing this. There seems no benefit. Your references have no value to me."

He appeared calm, rose, left the table and returned to his apartment.

* * *

Boiling with fury, he poured himself a stiff whisky. Then the phone rang.

"Hi, its Mads. The Chairman just walked into the office, announced you'd been sacked and then fired me. Can I come over?"

He arrived twenty minutes later, accepted a drink and related his dismissal to Alex. He had been terminated for cause, without severance pay or notice and marched off the premises by two armed security guards. The Corporate Secretary had handed him a letter and a copy of an email he had shared with an outside company. It made disparaging comments about three of the directors working on a project with the consultant.

"Can they use my emails this way Alex?"

"Yes. Anything sent using company equipment is open to them to read and use against you. You should have known better."

"Well I guess I did. I just got too relaxed about things. How about you? Can they really fire you without giving reasons?"

Alex gave a hollow laugh and poured himself another drink.

"There are many US states with 'at-will' termination clauses. New York's another. I've used them myself. If you give reasons, clever lawyers can challenge the justification. In most cases, the employer offers some decent terms to avoid a suit for wrongful dismissal. If it gets to court, US jurors usually find for the employee, especially if they are minority or female. Damages can be ridiculously high. Most jurors have been fired, or resent employers for other reasons. Such jurors would have no sympathy for a fat cat like me and not much more for a man on the rise like you."

"So, what will you do now Alex? I assume you'll go after the restoration of your shares?"

"I'm not bothered about the shares. Let them enjoy their ill-gotten gains. What will I do? Same as last time

I guess. I feel like murdering them, but a while in Buddhist meditation might help. How about you?"

"I'll do the same."

They discussed ideas and agreed they had best go to different locations. It would be a distraction to have a friend as a permanent reminder of KWZ in the same place.

Mads determined to head for a remote mountain in Nepal. There was a monastery run by Tibetan Monks he had heard about.

Alex decided to put almost all his wealth in trust for various charities. He planned to seek a group of Theravada forest monks in Thailand. He chose this branch of Buddhism because it focused on the earliest known teachings of the Buddha. He had deliberately selected a more remote location this time. No one would bother him there.

Mads' destination was a sect founded in the Eighth Century. It included many mystical and tantric practices. Alex viewed them as superstitions.

* * *

After three years in Thailand, Alex was able to meditate, cross-legged for days at a time. The initial pains from the fixed position, no longer distracted him. He only took breaks for light food, his toilet needs and deeply troubled slumbers.

He focused almost entirely on the Metta meditation, translated as "Loving Kindness." It offered a possible route to overcoming his seething anger. His dreams were full of fury against Alice, Lee-Soames and the other wicked self-serving monsters he had encountered in business.

The first stage of the meditation required him to forgive himself of his past mistakes and to be comfortable with himself. In the early days, this resulted in cold sweats and horrible visions of his first wife, Morag's suffering and death. He felt he caused this through his self-ish focus on work, his long absences and his affairs. He saw his daughters turning their back on him forever.

Sometimes, the meditation brought him to Argentina. He had cold-bloodedly killed the guards and technicians in Buenos Aires to complete his mission. Then, he had pushed his French ex-girlfriend under a bus. She was armed and trying to hand him over to the French Embassy. He dispatched a platoon of mountain troops during his arduous and perilous escape across the Andes.

He relived these scenes over and over. He could hear the screams, the cracking bones, the blood, the gunfire and the snuffing out of lives. How could he ever forgive himself? He came to realize that for all their Zen pretensions, true warriors saw their purpose as slaughter and death. This was the error of Bushido, the way of the warrior, adopted by the Japanese before World War II and wrongly endorsed by famous Zen monks. He shook with tears of self-disgust. The headaches began. They persisted every night.

With advice from his Australian mentor he came to accept what he had done, even his failure to defend Becky, the love of his life. She had taken bullets meant for him. The turbulent dreams and headaches became less frequent.

He found the second stage of the Metta meditation less traumatic. He was required to wish happiness, health, safety and contentment for a good friend. Often, he chose to think of the stalwart Mads, a fellow Buddhist. He had been a trusted helper in building better businesses for the benefit of all involved. Other times, Alex delved back into his time at university and thought of his friend and mentor Jock. *I've been blessed with several true friends.* He thought of Jaimie who had introduced him to the Marines and less happily to KZW.

In forgiving them their frailties and weaknesses, he gained further insights into his own limitations. He even brought to mind the rascally, but funny, Hamish. *My life is a pattern of interactions with others. If you live skillfully you can empathize with their needs, bring out the good in people and avoid doing harm.* Now, he saw his lack of skill in the past. The result had been pain and suffering for many, including himself.

The third stage was the simplest. He brought to mind a person he knew as an acquaintance. Some days he thought of the wizened old monk who swept the corridors of the monastery. He always smiled at Alex, but seemed to be profoundly deaf. Other days, he considered a porter in his Oxford college, or the geek who attended to his IT needs at Kendrick. *It's easy to wish them safety from harm, wellness, and happiness.*

If the first stage of forgiving himself had been a struggle, the fourth was really troublesome. It was about forgiving his enemies. For most of the minor ones it was easy. Even his torturer in Argentina, the Nazi officer in the remote snowbound house, was relatively simple. Perhaps this was because Alex had left him to a slow death. The man's blood stained the snow red, as Alex skied away. The really difficult enemies were, Alice, Lee-Soames and others. *How can I forgive, the despicable Hatchet-man from Kendrick consultants. This monster gloried in firing lowly workers featured large. Even worse was the evil John, the Pit-bull from Goldring Silverblatt, a truly horrible man.*

When Alex's Thai improved, the Abbot himself tutored Alex during this difficult stage. He explained that the skill was envisioning why these people were the way they were. By standing in their shoes Alex might understand them. Thinking of what upbringing they may have experienced is a start. He knew himself that a harsh father could cause great psychological damage. *I was lucky. Dad was not an alcoholic, a drug addict, a wife-beater or a thief. He taught me to be strong and independent.* His mentor taught him that genetic factors or head trauma could induce psychopathy. *Mmm, intellectually, I can see that their evil behaviors were not these people's fault. How I feel about it in my heart is entirely different.*

Frequently, his thoughts drifted into daydreams of torture and revenge.

He knew full well that hatred was harmful to himself. Time and again he tried to understand their feelings and motivations. It took him the best part of the third year to feel love for his enemies. Even then, his anger might break out from time to time.

The last segment in the process was to wish kindness to all living beings. This is why righteous Buddhists are vegetarians and save spiders that crawl into their houses. They live by precepts of doing nothing to harm or hurt other beings. They see themselves as one with all life.

Some days Alex felt himself close to ecstasy. He felt so much understanding for all beings. They were a part of the infinite universe, as he was himself. Other days, he lapsed back into old angst and self-blame.

* * *

In the fourth year, Alex took to meditating more during strolls along the forest pathways. *I like the feel of different*

textures of the tracks on my toes and the soles of my bare feet.
There was the soft dampness of wet leaves. Other days, he luxuriated in the dry dust and different stones. The sensations were constantly changing. Some stones were sharp. Others were worn smooth by the steps of generations of monks. *Each tread, each movement of all the walking bones focuses my mind.* The waving of trees bent by the breeze, the glistening dew on a dark green leaf, the fluttering of the blue butterfly's wings, the scurrying of an animal in the brush; all led him to delight in the unity and cycle of existence.

He began to contemplate other Buddhist teachings. He had always considered the widespread belief in Karma among Asian Buddhists as strange. *My intellect tells me that every action and every event causes results that resonate into the future. If I harm someone, the bad karma impacts the loved ones of that person in untold ways and for an untold time.*

He rejected the simple idea of reincarnation, in which 95% of Buddhist seemed to believe. *The idea of coming back to life on earth as another creature seems silly. On the other hand, I can easily envision the fluids and dust of my remains being recycled into the endless vastness of the universe.*

As he neared the end of his fourth year, he had achieved a calmness and equanimity he had never thought possible. He felt no desire for revenge. Instead, he had a deep understanding of himself and others. He began to wonder, *What good can I still do for others in the world outside?* An idea began to form in his mind. He discussed his ideas with the Abbot.

"You are in error. You should stay here longer."

Alex was unconvinced. He prepared to go forth and save the world.

CHAPTER TWENTY-TWO

The Pleasures of Yachting

"Lust is a many splendored thing."

What Shakespeare meant to say

Not long after Alex had these thoughts, Roberts of MI5 and Judd of MI6 were at their regular table in London's Special Forces Club. As Judd tucked into his roast beef and Yorkshire pudding, Roberts related the details of the call he'd received from the FBI.

"They want to put Alex in the frame for another murder. I told them that as far as we knew he was in Thailand. They say a year ago, the CIA sent some assets into the area where they thought he was. They never came back. Apparently, it's crawling with drug traffickers, war lords and other trigger happy types."

Judd Smirked.

"Bunch of amateurs. That rather serves them right don't you think? Ever since they smuggled heroin in the coffins of their troops from Vietnam into the States to fund their monkey business, the war on drugs has been out of hand. What the hell do they want from us?

"They just asked if we knew anything. I said no, but we'd inform them of any developments if they kept us in the loop. Well, let's get the full details of the murder and put some feelers out. There've been too many coincidences around Alex. The good doctor Maria Ramirez is still out there. We received an unconfirmed report that she was hired by a Burmese war lord to take out a rival. That puts her near Alex. Maybe she is behind this once more. Remember, she tried to steer blame onto Alex over Ted Barger's murder. She really has it in for him."

Robert's paused in his meal.

"Ah, 'Hell hath no fury' and all that."

* * *

In the jungles around Alex's hidden Monastery, Maria nearly came unstuck. She spent months thrashing around on false tails. An incident with a tiger left her with a dead guide and a deep gash in her arm. This developed into a fevered coma lasting weeks in a remote village. The skill of the shaman saved the limb and slowly brought her back to life.

She repaid the villagers by leaving no one alive. The straw-roofed huts burned fiercely, as she walked away along a muddy road. Voracious insects swarmed around, feasting on the corpses. She would steal a motorbike as soon as she met an unlucky traveler.

* * *

John Bastrami, the Pit-bull and now the Chairman of Goldring Silverblatt, sat in the cockpit of his 80-foot sail boat. He also owned a massive 300-foot ocean cruiser. That craft had all the trappings of riches and paranoia, including two helicopters. There was an extendable beach at the stern and much more.

He still preferred wind power best of all. As the spinnaker billowed from the prow, he gloated over his success. As Chairman of Goldring Silverblatt, he now possessed wealth and power beyond his early imaginings.

He steered the boat as he governed his global empire, with a firm hand. Taking advantage of the breeze, he tacked through the jagged dangers of the reef surrounding his private island. He liked to cruise around other islands in this Caribbean chain. He reveled in the salt on the wind, the cooling water droplets on his skin and the churning white wake under a clear blue sea.

His ex-Navy Seal body guard stood firmly on the foredeck. His biceps rippled as he scanned the horizon with binoculars. Occasionally, he stepped down into the cockpit, removing his shades to check the radar. The Pit-bull had ten of the Seal's comrades guarding his island. Since a bomb blast had killed Pit-bull's predecessor in his Connecticut home, he insisted on being closely guarded. His fears were exacerbated by the text that mysteriously appeared on his secure computer. It listed several of his crimes he thought only he knew about and baldly stated,

"You are the way you are because of your genes, upbringing and experiences. The evil you do harms millions, but is not your fault. You will be dealt with to prevent further suffering to others. It is your karma."

His IT security team traced the source to St Petersburg in Russia. They pointed out that the route had been complex and the message could have originated anywhere.

Pit-bull's power reached to deciding the futures of rulers and a strong influence on the new US president. The elites of the world feasted on the dealings and wealth of Goldring. Enemies must be eliminated and his person protected. Whenever he sailed, a helicopter was on a one-minute standby to dash to his rescue if there were any difficulties. The two choppers on the island were armed with M134 Mini-guns and missiles. Even his sail boat carried various hidden weapons. These included a hand held FIM-92 Stinger anti-aircraft rocket system, stashed near to hand.

He navigated towards one of his favorite palm fringed islands. He often found new delights there. His guard scanned the beach as they approached a cove on the far side. Pit-bull was annoyed to see a small motor cruiser occupying his preferred anchorage.

Impatiently, he grabbed the binoculars from his man. Then he relaxed and smiled. A near-naked beauty stood up, boldly looking back at him.

She had the dusky looks of a local girl. Her Afro hair and muscular long legs were complemented with huge breasts, barely restrained by a red bikini. His heart beat faster. He steered closer. The guard rolled his eyes. She waved.

He called out as they drew near.

"Come over. I'll send my man for you in the dingy."

He gestured to the tiny craft hanging from the stern. She shook her head. Her voice was husky with promise. She had a sexy local patois. He became aroused.

"No mon. It safer if yo com here. Leave the big mon on yo boat. I got rum and ganja."

The ex-Seal was instantly alert. He scanned the other boat and then the shore line. He was about to protest. His boss put a hand on his arm.

"You worry too much. You stay here."

Stripping off his shirt he dove into the water and swam over at a fast crawl. The warm water felt good. Full of anticipated pleasures, he hauled himself aboard. She gave him a look to melt metal. Leading him by the hand, she pulled him down into the cabin. He saw a bed and two rum cocktails on a table. He was about to reach out for her. She made an excuse for a delay and stepped back onto the deck. Under the cover of the cabin, she slipped into the water, out of site of the guard.

Puzzled, Pit-bull reached to go back through the door. There was the click of a lock. He banged on it. He tried the portholes. All were locked. He heard a voice from a speaker in the cabin. He thought he recognized it. He was terrified.

"Sit down John."

He did, wondering what could be next. A smell of gasoline leaked into the cabin. He scrabbled at the door in horror, screaming. As though his nemesis could hear him. He shouted.

"No! No!"

The Seal saw something in the water. He jerked into action, reaching for an M15 he had at hand. He could not believe the flash. He was knocked backwards by the searing shockwave of the explosion.

The girl looked back from the screen of trees. The fireball receded. The boat was blazing down to the water line. It billowed smoke. She muttered.

"Bumba cat yo done."

She scampered off into the undergrowth, retrieving a bag. It contained five thousand dollars and a blond wig. She straddled a concealed motorbike and rode off along a hidden track. She met her paymaster a mile further along. The figure, clad in black and masked, leapt on behind her. They abandoned the bike and jumped aboard a small speed boat. As they made their escape, the assassin dropped a spotter scope over the side. This was followed by the cell phone used to trigger the explosion. Both sank out of site into deep water.

* * *

Judd, Roberts and many others were summoned to the British foreign office. The normally cool new Foreign

Secretary sounded near to panic. Tubby and white-mop-headed, he was especially vociferous today. Waving his arms about and spluttering; he demanded,

"Who the hell knows what's going on? The Prime Minister just got reamed out by the President. He's accusing us of having something to do with killing the head of Goldring Silverblatt. Come on, speak up. Heads will roll for this. The bloody President hates me all ready. I want action this day!"

* * *

Breaching Thai and Burmese sovereign airspace, a CIA stealth drone flew at 45,000 feet over the Golden Triangle. Close ups of the Hidden Temple were streamed right into the War Room beneath the White House. The crosshairs hovered over the main building. A swarm of smaller drones, released earlier from the mother aircraft, showed the chanting monks within.

Impatiently, the President asked.

"Is the pale one him?"

The Director of the CIA answered.

"We're not sure Mr. President. The Brits say he may not even be responsible."

"Well just kill em all. Now! You can't trust the Brits, sneaky bastards."

The CIA drone pilot, safe in a concrete bunker in Texas, fired a Hellfire missile. The nose camera tracked it to the target. The temple was obliterated in a cloud of billowing smoke and flying debris.

The drone stayed on station. Five minutes later, three figures converged on the ruins. A fourth could be seen crawling out of the building.

The President did not wait for discussion. Tearing his eyes from a lustful look at a passing female Air Force colonel, he exclaimed,

"Bomb the slitty-eyed fuckers."

The second Hellfire finished the job. A thousand-year-old holy place and its community of peaceful monks had vanished in seconds.

The drone Pilot sipped his Coke.

CHAPTER TWENTY-THREE

Fitting Endings

"There is no satisfaction in vengeance unless the offender has time to realize who it is that strikes him and why retribution has come upon him."

Arthur Conan Doyle

In China a thousand years ago, the holy monk Linquan's mind left this earth. He was so revered by his community that his mummified body was posed in cross-legged meditation. They carefully wrapped his remains in a form of plaster. They covered it in go_d. He was set in eternal contemplation among the other Buddhist statues.

For hundreds of years, devotees meditated on the idea that his inspiration could lead them to nirvana. Over time, the memory of the mummification was lost. He became just another golden image in the temple.

During one of the periodic persecutions, the statue was hidden. In the 21st Century, archaeologists were amazed when X-rays revealed the hidden skeleton posed in prayer. Similar examples were discovered around China and in Japan.

* * *

Judd and Roberts bounced around in the van carrying them. Their hands and feet were bound with polymer restraints. These were of the type used to bundle computer wires together, only much stronger. Duct tape over their mouths prevented them calling out. Hoods blacked out their vision. They bumped into each other, as the vehicle cornered. Neither knew the identity of the other fleshy body.

As trained operatives, they tried to count the turns and estimate the speed along the straights. They could not remember being taken, but it must have been with drugs. Escape and evade was on their minds.

The van stopped. They heard the rear doors open. Rather gently, someone lifted them onto metal chairs in an abandoned warehouse. These were bolted to the floor. The hoods were whipped off by unseen hands from behind. They recognized each other, eyes wide with fear. Pictures and film clips appeared on a large screen in front of them. They were of people affected by the violence and suffering caused by the British all over the world. They saw dead children, slaughtered villagers and smoldering, bombed cities. It was all in graphic detail. The sound track was deafening. It comprised heart-tearing screams, wailing and despair.

Both men knitted their brows in puzzlement at the next film. It showed the discovery of Linquan's skeleton inside the golden statue.

An electric motor whirred as the screen rolled up into the ceiling. Before them were two wire frames in meditation position. They imagined what was coming. They thrashed around desperately, hopelessly. Their bonds cut into their wrists.

Each was sedated with an injection. They remained fully conscious. The restraints and gags were removed. They could neither speak nor move.

A masked figure in black carefully fitted each inside a wire frame. There was no pain as their legs were forced into the unfamiliar full lotus pose. The plaster covered wrapping began. A breathing tube was inserted and eye slits left open. Each wondered, was this Ramirez pointing the blame, or could it be Alex? Maybe the CIA had prematurely crowed over his death?

They could see their resplendent, gilded selves in a large mirror. They were swiveled round. The screen whirred back down. The same film of British evil was shown relentlessly, over and over. It drove them insane. After an interminable few days of starvation and thirst, they finally expired.

* * *

Alice Contessa-de Bracht, the Chairman of KZW consultants, sat at her computer in her Paris apartment. She considered the message on the screen, with haughty amusement. What lunatic had sent that? It listed some of the murders she had committed. There was a picture of the hidden torture chamber off her bedroom. Clips of the humiliation of many people came next. Included among them was the one she had showed the Board of KZW, featuring Alex. What was she supposed to make of the cryptic ending?

"You are the way you are because of your genes, upbringing and experiences. The evil you do harms millions, but is not your fault. You will be dealt with to prevent further suffering to others. This is your karma."

A professional killer would not send a warning. She pressed delete and smiled. She had her protection. Also, if anything happened to her, files would be sent to all the media. These would destroy the lives of hundreds of politicians, businessmen and others in high places all over the world.

* * *

Two weeks later, she was at her luxurious villa near Lake Maggiore in Northern Italy. She had a large estate there. Her private lake was a kilometer long and half that in width. The whole was surrounded by a high protective wall. Armed guards with fierce dogs patrolled the perimeter. What could be safer?

* * *

It was just after dawn. Her maid drove her in the electric golf cart. She stopped by the wooden jetty protruding into one end of the lake. As usual, Alice instructed the woman to return in an hour. She was bruised, cowed and frightened. She looked fearfully back at Alice as she drove away.

Alice dropped her robe and stood tall in her black La Perla swimsuit. On tiptoe, she stretched her arms above her head. Every muscle was toned. Her body reflected her former status as an Olympic swimmer. Regular exercise and Aikido kept her trim.

Her mind turned to the view. Snow-covered Alps and Switzerland rose as a majestic background. The far end of the lake remained in shade. Pines and undergrowth showed above a low carpet of mist over the water. She breathed in the chill air. With each inhalation, she luxuriated in its crisp purity.

Walking slowly to the end of the jetty, she paused. Expertly, she plunged in without a splash. The bracing shock of the icy water made her feel wholly alive. She loved to break the smooth glass of the liquid mirror. Expanding ripples moved slowly away from her.

The rhythm of her powerful breast stroke began. Thrust, kick, sweep, head up, breathe. Thrust, kick, sweep, head up, breathe. As her arms pushed ahead they shed tiny bubbles. Thrust, kick, sweep, head up, breathe.

Plowing forward, she relished her cleverness. She was an expert in corporate skullduggery. She used blackmail, charm and the elimination of rivals. Thrust, kick, sweep, head up, breathe. Maybe she would torture and make love with her maid when the girl returned.

Alice approached a shallow area near the middle of the lake. In the weeds a long, evil looking pike lay ready to dart out. It regarded her with a baleful yellow eye as she passed overhead. It was waiting in ambush, ready to dash out and seize any passing fish or water fowl. Its long snout was lined with vicious teeth.

Near the perimeter wall, several unconscious guards and tranquilized dogs lay sprawled at the edge of the woods. Hidden by the scrub at the far end of the water a black-clad figure slipped in unnoticed. An impeller on a small jetpack thrust him effortlessly towards the center of the lake.

Thrust, kick, sweep, head up, breathe. Alice spotted the approaching figure through her swimming goggles. She tensed. Taking a deep breath she decided to use her Aikido skills to deal with whoever it was.

Her wet-suited opponent stopped a few yards away. He drew a wicked looking spear gun from his back. Panicking, she turned. She swam away at a fast crawl. Her heart was pumping. She glanced over her shoulder. He was effortlessly following her.

She stopped and turned to face him, treading water. Maybe she could deflect the shaft? Recognizing her assailant through his face mask, she gasped in surprise. He fired the spear. Her blocking arm was too slow against the resistance of the water. Thud! The barb smashed into her midriff. A fat head, behind the point, burst through the hard muscles of her abdomen. A thin trickle of blood seeped from the wound. Her assailant backpedaled away a little, using his swim fins.

Alice could not feel her legs. Her spine must be broken. The figure in black gave a small wave with the fingers of one hand. With the other he pressed a button.

Boom! The explosive warhead blew Alice apart in a cloud of blood and pieces of flesh.

The green striped pike powered out from the weeds. Snapping up some bloody entrails, it dragged them backwards into its den.

CHAPTER TWENTY-FOUR

Happy Endings

"Bushido is achieved in the face of death. It means choosing death, if there is a choice between it and staying alive."

From Hagakure - The book of the Samurai - by Tsunetomo Yamamoto

Maria Ramirez was pissed off, as she leaned her Powerful Kawasaki hard into the ascending alpine curves. She tracked Alex around the world for weeks, using her contacts in Mossad and the Direction Générale de la Sécurité Extérieure. Their information led her to Alice's villa only an hour late. By the time she established that Alex was gone, she was nearly caught up in a massive police sweep. Her escape necessitated a rough ride through thick forests.

She was so close to Alex. She could taste her revenge. One final effort and she would have closure.

* * *

Algy Smythe, aka Hatchet-man's ruthless determination had driven him to be in charge of the whole of Kendrick and Co's European consulting activities. He was newly based in the regional headquarters in Munich.

It was late Friday evening and he waited expectantly in his office. Just his long-suffering secretary and the entrance security guards on the premises. The days when the Germans worked a full five-day week were long gone. Most of his colleagues had left by noon or earlier. They were off to summer parties, skiing in the nearby mountains or games of golf.

Hatchet-man was looking forward to meeting the reclusive, wealthy and incredibly rich Count Von Blauerach. It was a pain, but the man had requested an 8:00

pm appointment. Still, such a request was not to be denied. He busied himself reading over the reports on his guest. They did not include the suspected hidden assets and companies in Lichtenstein. Still, there was enough to set Hatchet-man salivating at the potential opportunities.

At 7:45 pm, his office door opened abruptly. He looked up. His secretary was slumped over her desk. Concerned, he rose to his feet, but an immaculately suited Alex waved him back into his chair. The black bore of a sawn-off shotgun waved menacingly around his midriff. He gulped and croaked out,

"Alex, what are you doing here? Point that thing away."

"Shut up Algy. I'm going to be busy, then we'll have a little chat."

Expertly, Alex taped his victim's hands to the arms of his chair and his feet to its base. He spun him round so he could not see the door.

He retrieved a back-pack from near the secretary's desk. Then, he set to work. Hatchet-man could hear various clicks, the unrolling of duct tape and other mysterious noises.

After ten minutes of this he heard the heavy door click shut. Alex spun him to face the door.

"Now you listen. Just nod if you understand me or I'll chop something off, every time you speak."

Hatchet-man was sweating. He nodded, eyes wide with fear. He let out a low whimper as Alex carelessly dropped the shotgun onto a side table. He calmly pulled out a razor sharp wakizashi. The Samurai short sword was ideal to fill his threat. It was the traditional weapon used in the suicide ritual Sepuku.

Alex kept looking at his watch as he harangued his prisoner. He told him of the harm he had done to millions of working people and their families. He required frequent fearful nods of the head. He told Algy of his utter lack of empathy, his monstrous gloating over his tally of terminations, and much more.

Alex's phone beeped, alerting him to something. He looked pleased. The beeps became more frequent.

Finally, he neared an end of his monologue. He raised the weapon to head height.

"You know, there are much worse things than dying Algy. Living with a constant recollection of horror is far worse. Death brings peace."

Alex stood silently, letting his words sink in. He turned his thoughts inward. He brought to mind the vivid images of the monk Qwang Duc, venerable abbot of a monastery in Hoy An, Vietnam. Once seen the film clip can never be forgotten. The holy man protested against the corrupt South Vietnamese government during the war. In the middle of a main road, he poured

gasoline over himself. As the flames caused his meditation pose to collapse, he stoically righted the arm that
had given way. This happened three times. Finally, he
expired in the flames.

Alex had always felt suicide went against the precept
of Buddhism, against taking life. His teachers told him
that such protests dated back to pre-Buddhist India. The
theory was that when a monk had reached a level of nirvana, he was ready to move to the next existence. So,
it was acceptable to speed the process as a protest. This
sounded like sophistry to Alex.

As he looked intently at his victim, Alex felt at peace
with everything. Now the phone was giving a continuing tone. Sensors he had set in the building were trig-
gered. He leaned forward to Hatchet-man, who instinc-
tively drew back. Then, in a smooth determined move
he drew the blade deep across his own throat. Blood
shot out in a huge spurt from the massive wound. It
sprayed everywhere. Hatchet-man screamed in horror.
He blinked to clear blood from his eyes. Alex teetered
for a second. Then he tumbled to the floor, his eyes glaz-
ing over.

Hatchet-man gave a roar of triumph. He would remember this scene. It would be one of joy rather than
terror. Why should he care that a lunatic killed himself?

Just as he was congratulating himself on survival, the
door burst inwards. Ramirez and two thugs fanned out

in the room, waving their MP5 assault guns. She saw the bloody corpse. Kneeling by it, she felt thwarted. It was puzzling.

A thought caused her to swing round and face the door. No! Alex had led her here at exactly this time. The text from the Hatchet-man must have been hacked. The explosion of two kilos of plastic explosive from the door blew everything in the room to smithereens. The external window billowed outwards in a cloud of debris and smoke.

* * *

It was early, before sunrise in Nepal. Mads Petersen was meditating cross-legged in the snow on a mountain peak. He wore only a light robe. He should have been frozen solid an hour earlier. He had learned to focus heat and the blood flow around his vital organs and brain. The rest went into a type of hibernation.

His heart jolted. The trance was broken. He felt the death of Alex as a huge pain in his stomach. The sensation changed. He sensed Alex's inner calm and fulfillment before he faded away.

The End

ABOUT THE AUTHOR

Aaron Aalborg is the penname of a writer with many and varied experiences. He chooses to remain anonymous. Born in the North of England, he has variously been a trainee Catholic monk, a student activist, a Royal Marine Commando, a visiting Professor at a European Business School and a successful businessman and global CEO. He and his wife have lived in Asia, Europe and the US. This included travel to all the major and many smaller countries, doing business in most of them. He currently resides in Central America and is a Buddhist (a rather bad one).

Aaron's books are intended to provoke thought and challenge the status quo, as well as to entertain and excite.

On behalf of the author and Penman House Publishing, Thank you. We appreciate your support.

Reviews are the life's blood of publishers, authors and help inform other readers. They act as signposts on the literary landscape.

Please take a moment and leave a review of this book on Amazon, GoodReads or wherever readers gather.

Contacting our Authors and Penman House

Our authors love to receive feedback and to engage with readers

Aaron's email: Aaron@penmanhouse.com,

K Francis Ryan's: Ryan@penmanhouse.com.

Michael Crump's: Michael@penmanhouse.com

Penman House publishing's website is: http://www.penmanhouse.com/

There is much information, news and other material useful to readers and writers there, including **Aaron's blog,** book reviews, poems and much more.

Message to Book Clubs

Our authors like to work with book clubs. So far, this has included live or post event interaction using Facebook or other media. If you wish to discuss this, please email the appropriate author, see above.

OTHER BOOKS FROM PENMAN HOUSE PUBLISHING

Aaron Aalborg

Terminated Volume 1
From the Slums to the Falklands War

Currently Available

Revelations from recently declassified government archives drive the start of this thriller in two parts. Alex, a talented lad from the most deprived part of Scotland, overcomes the disadvantages of his birth to play a key role in Britain's victory over Argentina in the Falklands war.

He also becomes a successful businessman. The corruption and evils of corporate life are exposed through a series of exciting events.

Terminated is for those who like cliff-hanging thrillers and anyone interested in the world of big business, management consulting and war.

Cooking the Rich

Currently Available

A Post Revolutionary Necessity – A spoof cookbook of jokey recipes. It skewers politicians and the undeserving rich with humor and insight.

Recipes include:

Trump a la mode

Real Windsor Soup

Murdoch stew and many others

It includes amusing graces and other whimsy

Doom Gloom and Despair

Currently Available

A collection of apocalyptic short stories, with dark humor, but serious overtones.

These include:

A tale of how a dog feels about being taken to the vet for castration and his subsequent revenge.

The catastrophic and cannibalistic results of a massive volcanic eruption in Central America.

A plot to drastically solve overpopulation and climate change by the combined military of the major powers.

A universe destroying scientific catastrophe.

Good and Evil Gods dueling with our planet.

And many more.

They Deserved It

Currently Available

A novel of lust and Revenge Spanning the Centuries.

What is the mysterious Egyptian casket that links murderers over a thousand years?

This thriller begins as a historical novel set in 17th Century Italy, a time of superstition, plagues and cynical exploitation of young women.

It is a ripping yarn of illicit love, hundreds of poisonings, the inquisition, torture and witch burnings, built around true events.

Characters include: beautiful girls oppressed by dynastic marriages to aged husbands, an attractive and tormented young priest, Machiavellian cardinals and a scheming atheist pope.

In the second part of the story, the descendants of some of the original characters are driven to fulfill their ancestral destiny in modern day New York. The results include: grisly killings, global pursuit, international espionage and a thrilling climax of mass murder, authorized by the President of the United States.

It is up to you to decide which of the victims deserved their fate.

Revolution

Currently Available

A thriller to change the world.

This is a must read novel for anyone who really wants to change the way the world is run. It describes a violent revolution in the near future. It begins in the United Kingdom and blossoms into worldwide mayhem.

Three students are radicalized in the late 1960s. After violent experiences, they bide their time till they are in positions of power. They assassinate members of the British Royal family and world leaders, before seizing control in a series of credible and stunning acts of violence. With the President dead, the upheaval spreads to the US and throughout the world.

Counter-revolutionaries attempt to strike back. This is a frighteningly realistic view of what could happen in today's uncertain and dangerous times. It is of compelling interest to those of the political left and right, military specialists, radical economists and all those who enjoy a twisting turning plot with many surprises.

BloodAxe -
The saga of 20th Century Wannabe Vikings

Coming Later this Year

A group of crusty old men decide they would like to be Vikings. This starts with harmless reenactments and ends with the slaughter and pillaging of a modern-day English village. Fun, thrills, excitement and extremely black humor.

K. Francis Ryan

The Echoes Quartet

An adult paranormal mystery series set in the present.

Echoes Through the Mist

Currently Available

Julian Blessing's high-octane Wall Street career is likely to land him in prison. The economy is rapidly melting down. His ex-wife wants him dead and some Russian mobsters share her sentiments. And that's just today.

Julian thinks now would be the right time to start listening to the voice only he hears. The words Julian hears bring a message as emphatic as it is baffling and propels him to a village on the rugged coast of Ireland.

A madman possessing supernatural powers wants to sow terror in the hearts of those in the village. His craving for revenge and his limitless greed put Julian directly in his path. By protecting the village, Julian puts himself high on the madman's to-be-slaughtered list.

Desperate for any advantage, Julian discovers the Hagan, a woman with vast supernatural gifts who is steeped in Ireland's ancient wisdom. Hers are otherworldly talents with decidedly this-worldly applications.

Victims are multiplying fast as Julian races to unlock the Hagan's mysterious arts. Her arcane knowledge is the only hope he has of drawing his fellow villagers back from annihilation.

To stay alive long enough to use what he learns, Julian must trust his heart to a stranger, his soul to a witch and place his life in the hands of a village full of Irish lunatics.

Echoes Through the Vatican

Currently Available

A shadow organization, tracing its dark ancestry back two thousand years, wants only one thing from Julian–Assassinate the Pope, the leader of 1.2 billion Roman Catholics.

A corrupt cardinal, an honorable priest, a sadistic mobster, a whorehouse madam and a stymied police inspector–They all want something and that something is Julian Blessing.

The loss of everything Julian would give up his life to protect is the outcome if he fails to navigate the deadly maze of Vatican intrigue.

With everything at stake, what if you lose? And what of the Jesuit Book?

Echoes From the Past

Currently Available

Terrorist bombings, political unrest and a man whose life is in tatters…

Julian, a man with exceptional paranormal powers is back in Ireland to face his most daunting challenge yet.

The Jesuit Book–It is a book that some say doesn't exist. Others are afraid to admit it does. Others will murder to get it. Julian is the keeper of the Book. His task is to protect regardless of risks, heedless of the costs.

During his mission to Rome, friends died and others wish they had. Badly scarred emotionally, Julian has returned to Ireland to rebuild himself as well as prepare for the conflict he knows will come. Can he overcome his own demons in order to fight those who would take the Book and his life?

Echoes Through Time

Coming Soon

Michael Crump

El Peón: And Other Stories From the Campo

Currently Available

Three young children from the same family grow up in the violent and rapidly changing Central America of the 1980's and 90's. Haunted by their own family trauma each child struggles to make a life. Includes six short stories of historical and cultural interest set in Central America.

Candyman's War

Currently Available

A young graduate student returns to his family's home in Guatemala to find

The Civil War at its peak in 1982. Traumatized by what he sees in the Indigenous villages, he joins the guerillas and rapidly rises to a position of leadership. His short but violent "war" culminates in a major setback for the government and a startling life change for himself

Oligarch

Currently Available

A young German immigrates to Guatemala in 1936 to escape the holocaust. He builds a coffee farm and marries into an oligarch family. Rejected by other Germans because of his Jewishness and eventually alienated from his wife's family because of his socialism, he raises a family that is sympathetic to the plight of the indigenous Mayans. The story begins with his son, Dr. Wilhelm who returns from medical school to take up the fight against the government in 1974.

Riley Smythe

Eleven Days

Currently Available

William (Wilhelm) Hoffman from The Oligarch and his Mayan wife, Elena fled Guatemala in 1982 when Elena was pregnant with Lela Itzel. Just after the cease-fire, they return in 1998 with Lela for the funeral of William's aunt Dolores who has used her share of the family's estate to support excavations of massacre sites. She, along with others (Bishop Gerardi) has been murdered. Before she died she set up a situation in which the sixteen-year-old Lela Itzel would be pursued by the government. The chase includes old friends and enemies of William and Elena in a hair-raising and ultimately maturing experience for Lela.

Three Degrees

Coming Soon

Lela Itzel, now in college in the US accepts an internship with a small newspaper in order to spend the summer with her boyfriend. He's in trouble when she gets there and soon she is too.

All titles are sold exclusively through Amazon and are available in E-book and paperback.